"You're not seriously thinking of keeping me here!" she cried

"I'm sorry it's come to this, Mandy, but you need protection."

With a strangled cry Mandy ran for the door to find a telephone. But she fell into Pascal's arms instead and he wrapped them around her like the coils of an iron snake.

"Let me go!" she yelled.

"Save your breath," he said levelly. "Or I'll stop it for you!"

"How?"

He stopped. Stared at her, his eyes glowing. She gasped, sensing the flare of his sexual desire as she gazed up at him. Clutched to his chest, she became intensely aware of him. The way his heart beat beneath her hand.

He bent his head in a sudden movement, and kissed her.

Dear Reader,

Welcome to Sara Wood's colorful new trilogy. The series is full of family intrigue, secrets, lies and, of course, love. It involves the St. Honoré family, which has a reputation second to none in Saint Lucia. Mandy, Ginny and Amber are about to be drawn into this notorious family and the secrets of its past. Each of these intrepid heroines is looking for love and each of them will find it—but only where they least expect it! But then, as you'll discover, in this series things are rarely as they seem!

In *White Lies*, Mandy Cook is desperate to find her father, and perhaps Vincente St. Honoré can help her. If she can ever find him! For first she must wrest herself from the arms of his commanding and charismatic son—Pascal.

In *Scarlet Lady* (#1916), Ginny MacKenzie is a successful fashion model, but her worst nightmares are confirmed as she is wrongly branded a scarlet lady by the press and loses her husband, the Hon. Leo Brandon, as a result. It is only when, two years later, she decides to search for love elsewhere that Ginny is reunited in Saint Lucia with the man she has always loved—Leo! The question is, why is he there? You can read Ginny's story in October 1997.

In *Amber's Wedding* (#1922), Amber Fraser has just married Jake Cavendish, not for love but for convenience, companionship and to secure a father for her unborn child. On their wedding day Jake reveals to Amber a secret that will change her life. A secret that will finally reveal the truth about the St. Honoré family. They honeymoon in Saint Lucia where love appears to blossom after all—until Amber discovers Jake's real motive for marrying her. You can read Amber's story in November 1997.

Happy reading!

The Editor

SARA WOOD

WOOD

White Lies

Harlequin Books

TORONTO • NEW YORK • LONDON
AMSTERDAM • PARIS • SYDNEY • HAMBURG
STOCKHOLM • ATHENS • TOKYO • MILAN
MADRID • WARSAW • BUDAPEST • AUCKLAND

ISBN 0-373-11910-0

WHITE LIES

First North American Publication 1997.

With my grateful thanks to Mrs. Joan Devaux,
Gary Devaux, Maria Monplaisir and
all at Anse Chastanet

CAST OF CHARACTERS

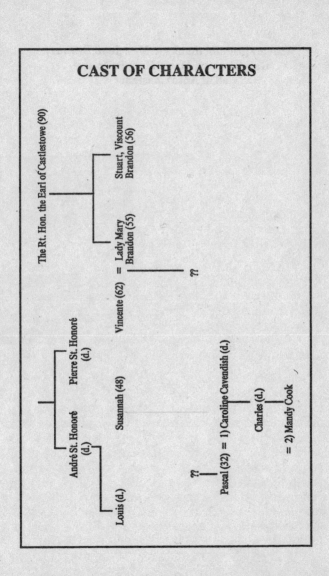

CHAPTER ONE

'THE... Caribbean?' repeated Mandy incredulously.
'There must be some mistake! I can't possibly have any
family there! I thought,' she said, suddenly more
subdued, 'that this was an advert from a relative who
was trying to trace me. That can't be right, can it?'

'Why not?' The solicitor smiled encouragingly.

In a wistful gesture that was almost a caress, her hand
smoothed the much read page of the newspaper in front
of her and she went over the words of the advert again,
even though she knew them by heart.

MANDY COOK, née Brandon. Born 26.8.71,
Sunnyside Nursing Home, Glasgow. Resident of West
Hill Children's Home, and St Mary's Children's
Home. Married David James Cook, 26.8.89. Last
heard of in Devon.

Please contact the office below where you will learn
something to your advantage.

Cold facts, simple words. And yet they'd aroused such
a disturbing turbulence in her that she'd barely been able
to keep her finger steady to dial the number given for
the London solicitor, Jack Lacey. Full of excitement and
hope, she'd gabbled out her story—that she'd been
searching for her natural parents for a long, long time
and was hardly daring to hope that she might have a
positive lead at last.

And luckily Jack Lacey had understood why she'd
been half laughing, half crying and why her words had
tumbled out in an unstoppable rush like a river in
full spate.

'Come at once,' he'd said. 'Take the next train from Plymouth.'

And here she was in his office, four hours later. She'd sipped tea and nervously chatted to him while he checked the documents she'd brought as proof of her identity.

Then he'd looked up and stunned her by saying that she was to fly to St Lucia in the Caribbean!

'I dearly want this to give me a link with my real parents,' she said earnestly. 'But it's so unlikely—'

Jack Lacey lifted a thick grey eyebrow. 'Is it? The details are correct, aren't they? I can understand your amazement, but my contact in St Lucia said that when I found Mandy Cook his client wanted her to take these tickets and make the trip to the West Indies as soon as possible.' He smiled at her, knowing that she desperately wanted to be convinced. 'I believe quite a few Scots went out to work on plantations in the past. Why not one of *your* relatives?'

Mandy found herself smiling back wryly. 'Because having exotic connections isn't the kind of thing that happens to ordinary people like me!'

A little dazed, she stared at the tickets in front of her. Heathrow to St Lucia. St Lucia to Heathrow. They were genuine; the solicitor had checked them out—and he'd confirmed that the hotel accommodation at the Anse La Verdure Hotel was genuine too.

'I can't think of anyone better,' said Jack Lacey gently. 'Go,' he urged. 'Treat yourself. I'll get in touch with Vincente St Honoré once I know your flight plans.'

'I could ring him from home, couldn't I?' she suggested cautiously. 'That would save his client's money.' And save herself a nerve-racking trip. Mandy flipped open the clasp of her handbag and began to rummage for something to write on. 'Do you have his phone number or address?'

'I'm not to divulge that,' Lacey said to her surprise. 'I know; odd, isn't it? But those are my instructions. He wants to contact *you*. If his client is willing to pay for your travel, why argue? I'm sure you'll be told everything when St Honoré meets you.'

It seemed very cloak-and-dagger. Why weren't people straightforward instead of being so devious? It could be a huge disappointment. It could be... oh, it would be wonderful if St Honoré could put her in touch with relatives.

'If he refers to a client, does that mean that Vincente St Honoré is a solicitor? If so, surely he would have said something about the purpose of the advert?' She leaned forward eagerly. 'It's worded as if someone's died and the executors are searching for anyone with claims on the estate. What do you think?'

Jack Lacey nodded. 'That's how I read it. But St Honoré has told me nothing. He could be just a lay executor, but he keeps referring to his "client" so I'd put my money on him being a solicitor as well. I assume he's acting as a go-between for someone and he wants to satisfy himself that you're who you say you are. However, I'd advise you not to raise your hopes—'

'Why?' Mandy asked quickly.

'Because he hinted that he was making other enquiries. That's all I know.' Lacey hesitated, seeing how her spirits had fallen and that the joy had vanished from her face. 'I wish I could tell you more.'

'I'm not interested in any financial gain,' Mandy said shakily. 'It's... it's the prospect of discovering my roots that's excited me. But if there are doubts...'

All of a sudden her voice became croaky with emotion and her soft hazel eyes grew filmy with unshed tears. Flying to St Lucia only to discover that there had been a mistake would be quite devastating to her. Disappointments had peppered all her attempts to find her family so far and increasingly she was afraid to allow hope into her heart any more—even though her quest was becoming an obsession.

Lacey cleared his throat. 'All I know is that St Honoré wants you in St Lucia.'

'For an audition, perhaps?' she asked with a rueful laugh. 'Or some kind of identity parade, where this man's client stands behind a two-way mirror and picks out whoever has the greatest family resemblance?'

'I don't know,' confessed Lacey, giving her a sympathetic grin. 'But if there's any doubt I'm sure DNA testing will be used if necessary, to put everyone's mind at rest. I hope it works out,' he added quietly. 'I'd hate to see you return disappointed.'

'I would be, Mr Lacey,' she said fervently. 'I've longed to know about my mother all my life.' She dropped her gaze for a brief moment. Jack Lacey's sympathetic eyes were encouraging her tears to form, and she knew that she mustn't let herself cry or she'd never feel tough enough to cope with the prospect of failure.

'See it as a holiday, all expenses paid,' he told her. 'I envy you, Mrs Cook. How about taking a personal advisor with you?' he suggested, a twinkle in his eyes.

She flashed him a grateful smile for realising that she needed a touch of humour to lift her spirits. 'I can't afford you! Besides, you'd miss your daughter's school play—and your wife's...what did you say? Her tip-tilted smile and the way she sings around the house.'

Jack Lacey laughed warmly. Unlikely though it seemed, the young woman in the washed-out, demure blue dress and the cheap shoes had totally disarmed him with her admiring exclamations over the photograph of his family and had somehow coaxed him to wax sentimental about the people he loved.

'You're right,' he admitted, feeling an odd affection for Mandy. He frowned. She was so open that she'd be extremely vulnerable. 'Don't get hurt,' he said suddenly, with fervour.

'How kind you are!' she said warmly. Her eyes shone with pleasure through the fine veil of tears. 'I might,' she admitted. 'I'm afraid that happens now and then. I trust people and sometimes they let me down. I've had cranks and opportunists answering my adverts and pretending to be a long-lost parent before, as I told you.'

'But no crank would fund a trip to the West Indies,' reasoned Jack Lacey.

'That's what I'm banking on,' she said eagerly. 'This time the solicitor in St Lucia *could* be acting for a relative of mine and I *might* learn about my past. I know it would be wiser not to get excited, but this means everything to me, Mr Lacey. If I find my mother, or my father, or even *one* relative, I'll come right back and hug you!'

Jack Lacey found himself praying that she would. But as she left, his hand aching from where she had squeezed it so fiercely and a lump in his throat at the quiet joy on her pale face, he thought of the ice-cold tones of the man he'd been told would contact her and he wondered if he should have warned her more strongly. He sighed, knowing that he wouldn't have had the heart.

Mandy Cook might discover that some families were best left divided and that the mother who'd abandoned her at the nursing home had probably had a good reason to keep her baby girl's existence a secret from her relatives.

'A Planter's Punch for you too, madam?'

Mandy smiled warmly at the woman who'd come to the table in the spacious, open-air lounge of the hotel. The 'welcome' drink looked long and cool and fruity—just what she needed after the hot and dusty drive.

She checked the name-tag on the frill decorating the woman's crisp white blouse. 'Please, Agnes,' she said gratefully. 'The road was so bumpy! I felt quite shaky when I got out of the minibus.' She took a sip of the drink and detected the faint taste of rum.

'It's bad,' agreed Agnes equably, and shot her a curious glance. 'Are you Mrs Cook?' And at Mandy's nod she said, 'Monsieur St Honoré's been asking after you.'

Mandy glowed with delight. 'Is he here?'

'He's on the beach,' Agnes said shortly. 'Simon will show you. Simon!'

'The *beach*?' Mandy quickly drained her glass and jumped up. She felt a little unsteady, but then she'd been sitting for hours and hours on the plane. She smiled at the young bar attendant who came running up. And she wondered how many St Lucian solicitors received their clients on the beach! 'The beach! It's wacky. I think I'm going to love Anse La Verdure,' she said with a grin.

'Everybody does. It's the best in the Caribbean,' said Simon proudly. He indicated the key in her hand. 'Would you like to unpack and rest first?' he asked thoughtfully, but then, they'd had a long chat already, and she'd drawn out half his family history from him.

She hesitated. Perhaps she ought to take the opportunity to freshen up and wait till her shakiness had gone before confronting the man she'd flown thousands of miles to see. But she was eager to meet him—and she felt sure that her dizziness would pass once her body had realised that it had stopped travelling.

'I'll be all right,' she said. 'I've had time to drop off my hand luggage.' She smiled, thinking happily of the luxurious villa perched higher up the hill. 'Mr St Honoré takes priority.'

'We go that way.' Simon pointed to some dark volcanic steps which led from the terrace of the bar and lounge area.

'OK. I'll see you all later, I expect,' she said warmly to the other guests sitting nearby, and they smiled and cheerfully lifted their glasses in a friendly farewell.

She followed the teenager down the steep hill, occasionally catching glimpses of an impossibly blue sea scintillating like a jewel in the hot sun. The steps wound through a tropical garden of palm trees, hibiscus, great billows of bougainvillea...

In answer to her request, Simon began to give her the names of the plants, shouting them over his shoulder—angels' tears, heart flower, water-well, paw-paw, mango, bottlebrush—till her mind reeled.

But it took the edge off her tense anticipation. Somewhere on the beach below was the man who might change her life. And as she hurried after the white-clad Simon her whole body almost bounced with joy till the thick brown rope of her plait bounced too in sympathy.

'Where is he?' At the bottom of the steps she paused to search the beach expectantly. Yet there was no one remotely like a solicitor in sight. 'I'm looking for a guy in a bowler hat and pinstriped suit with a briefcase,' she said with a chuckle. 'I suppose I've got that wrong!'

Simon grinned back at her. 'No suits here! Only sand and sea, sun and tanned people. Everybody having a good time.'

Mandy beamed merrily at all the friendly faces nearby and was rewarded with a battery of smiles in return. 'It's going to be so lovely staying at this hotel!' she sighed. 'I expected people to be standoffish. But they all look as happy as I feel.'

'Sure they do. This is paradise,' said Simon. He paused, then gave a satisfied exclamation. 'I see him! You follow me, lady!'

Excitedly Mandy strode after his eye-searing, white-clad figure, barely controlling her urge to skip. Her pulses, however, were galloping along in leaps and bounds because all her hopes and dreams were bound up in this moment. Even admiring the dazzling blue sky, the translucent sea and the 'desert island' beach with its leaning palms and sultry, tropical atmosphere came second to her long-term goal. Beaches she could enjoy later. The unbelievable view to the mountains from her balcony could be drooled over some other time. This was her future, after all.

Preoccupied by her thoughts, she stumbled on a ridge of sand. Seeing Simon's curious glance, she grinned and said, 'It's OK. I feel wobbly. I'm just nervous as a kitten about this meeting!'

Simon's step faltered. 'Monsieur St Honoré is—' He stopped, seemingly unable—or unwilling—to continue.

Mandy's joy faded a little. There seemed to be a kind of warning in Simon's silence. Feeling a little alarmed, she stopped and touched his arm. 'What is it?' she asked uncertainly. 'What's worrying you? He is here, isn't he?' Frantically she searched up and down the shoreline, her heart sinking. 'There isn't anyone with clothes on,' she said in wry disappointment, 'let alone a suit!'

'Monsieur St Honoré, he don't wear a suit often. Or many clothes much,' explained Simon.

'Not...wear...!' Her eyes widened. 'Where is he?'

'There!' Simon seemed embarrassed but she didn't have time to question him further because he added hastily, 'Monsieur St Honoré!'

He lay sprawled beneath the waving fronds of a nearby palm tree, sunlight and palm shadows contriving to slash his lithe form with gold and black. A sleeping tiger. A rather magnificent animal, the torso sculpted with firm muscle, the tanned body beautifully taut and lean. And he wasn't wearing much—only a pair of brief green bathing shorts, low on the narrow hips.

This was Monsieur St Honoré? A *lawyer*? Mandy put a hand to her mouth to stop her gasp of disbelief and tried to gather her wits. 'Simon, I think you've made a mistake—' she began in a hushed and urgent whisper.

'No mistake,' he replied, sounding hurt. 'This is him.'

For Simon's sake she gave the man another once-over. He looked thirtyish, his flaxen hair sun-streaked and with no hint of grey. It was untidy too, the thick, springing curls tousled and damp as though he'd recently been for a swim. Her uncertain gaze took in his thick, honey-coloured brows and his strong bone structure, high-lighted by the sun where it hit the prominent cheekbones and firm jawline.

OK, she thought. Solicitors came in all shapes and sizes. But... tousled? *Rakish?* Mandy now understood Simon's unstated warning. He looked the kind of man who'd bite.

'This is Monsieur St Honoré? You're absolutely *sure?*' she persisted in a whisper.

'Definitely,' the young man answered. 'This, Monsieur St Honoré. *That—*' and he pointed out to sea '—his boat.'

'Oh! Thanks,' she said absently, riveted by the sight of the boat.

Simon left her gaping at the sleek motor yacht lying a short distance off shore. Its size and elegant lines screamed money. She shaded her eyes against the glare from the sea and watched its launch being drawn up out of the water by an on-board crane.

'Wow!' she breathed. A crane on a boat! Even more astonishing was the sea-level bathing deck at the stern, where a couple of St Lucians in white shorts and shirts were setting up a barbecue—a barbecue! 'Now that is money! How the rich do live!' she marvelled.

The gold letters on the stern proclaimed the boat to be named *St Honoré*, confirming Simon's claim. Con-founded, Mandy followed the line of the mooring rope. It extended all the way to the beach where its end had been coiled a couple of times around a palm tree. The one that shaded the sleeping tiger.

Mandy moved closer, eyeing the teak-coloured body admiringly. It was too good a sight to ignore. His flat, muscle-defined stomach tensed slightly and she took a startled pace back, thinking for a crazy moment that he was aware of her presence despite the resolutely closed eyelids. Embarrassment made her pink and hot. Nice women didn't ogle men's bodies in public!

Then something dawned on her. He didn't look ready to conduct any business at all. There was just him and the sand and the palm tree. No briefcase, no shoes, no clothes, no towel. She swayed slightly and realised that the sun was beating down on her head. Cautiously she ducked under the shady palm and wondered what to do.

There had been some mistake. Her stomach turned over with the intense disappointment. Someone had got his wires crossed. Her soft eyes glazed over as she gloomily reviewed her situation and battled with the fear of failure.

Perhaps her hopes had been raised unnecessarily. All along she'd tried not to expect too much, just in case she was disappointed. But how could you *not* get excited at the prospect of finding a blood relative when you'd longed for family all your life?

And...maybe she'd be asked to pay back the cost of the ticket! Appalled, she lifted her eyes to the heavens. 'Oh, Lord!' she groaned aloud, swamped with misery. 'If this doesn't work out, I could be on the streets!'

Something shimmered at her feet, making her look down quickly. The man had stirred and stretched, sunlight bouncing off the planes and curves of his body and the wide bracelet of his gold watch. As she watched, holding her breath, the heavy fringe of golden lashes fluttered. So did her pulses and her stomach. And then she found herself pinned by the bluest and most compelling pair of eyes she'd ever seen.

'Hi,' said their owner lazily, bringing up an arm behind his head. And then the tiger stretched again, flexing and tensing a battery of shifting muscles in the process. Mandy half expected him to purr.

She cleared her throat. 'Hi.' And cleared it again because she'd sounded as if she was suffering from bronchitis. 'I was looking for Monsieur Vincente St

Honoré...' She paused and took a deep breath, her mouth trembling. Better get it over with. 'I don't think I've got the right man, have I?' she asked sadly.

He smiled. Not much, just enough to make the firm, male mouth quirk in a disconcertingly attractive curve. He'll bite! she reminded herself hastily.

'Expecting someone older?' he murmured.

For a moment she was taken aback by his silky, fascinating accent. And then, seeing his amused eyes on her, she found her voice again. 'Well, yes...'

'My father.'

'Oh! Mystery explained!' she said huskily. 'I thought there had been a mistake. I'm so relieved!'

'I bet.'

Mandy risked a friendly smile and tried to place the accent. French, presumably. Herbert, the man who'd driven the minibus from the airport, had said the British and French had fought endlessly over the island. Seven times British, seven times French.

It seemed to her that the man's sexy accent was mixed with the slow-blues drawl of the Caribbean, and it reached into her stomach like warm, soothing cocoa. Mandy concealed the weakening effect of the richly flowing voice and got down to business.

'I'm glad there's no mix-up,' she said in a rush. 'Mr Lacey told me Monsieur St Honoré would contact me—and then the girl at the bar said Monsieur St Honoré was waiting on the beach and then, when I saw you, well!' She laughed but he didn't smile in response and continued to gaze at her cynically. Her smile faded. 'I was sure something was wrong,' she said more soberly, 'and I didn't know what to do.'

He jackknifed his strong legs and stood up in a leisurely, languid way as if his joints had been oiled as comprehensively as his gleaming dark body. 'I'm Pascal.' Then he smiled and two dimples appeared in each cheek, utterly distracting her because they turned him from a rake into a charmer. 'You're Mandy Cook, I presume?'

'Yes!'

Everything was going to be all right! Overjoyed, Mandy took the offered hand enthusiastically. It was large and dry and strangely comforting, and it reminded her of her beloved Dave's hands so much that she was momentarily thrown off balance.

'Delighted,' he murmured. 'Absolutely delighted.'

And the frisson that Pascal St Honoré engendered was something new—a sudden contracting of her loins, and unexpected awareness of his sexuality. Startled, she flipped a quick glance up at the blue, blue eyes and then wished that she hadn't. He was studying her with a frank and open interest that left her wondering where her breath had gone.

'Thank goodness!' she burbled, letting her mouth take over. 'For a ghastly moment I thought I'd been the victim of a practical joke! I'd half expected someone with a bald head, a pinstriped suit and a briefcase, you see, and you didn't fit that bill at all so—'

'You're after my father.'

It sounded like a statement rather than a question. 'Yes,' she said eagerly. 'I—'

'How was the flight?' he enquired politely.

'Endless.' she grinned, forgiving him his constant interruptions. She had been gabbling on. Nerves seemed to have loosened her tongue. She sighed and tried to stay demure and decent. 'So was the drive from the airport. We took twenty minutes to do the last two miles! Those potholes in the road are unbelievable! My body's still swaying—'

'It is somewhat inaccessible here,' he conceded. 'But it keeps down the number of tourists on this end of the island.' His eyes seemed to mock her. 'A little discomfort is worth suffering if you end up with your dream, isn't it?' he drawled.

She nodded vigorously. 'I absolutely agree! I never mind hardship if there's something special at the end, as a reward.' There was an odd flicker in his eyes that made them briefly splinter with cold lights and then he was smiling again. 'I suppose you're used to travelling on that road. It joggled every bone in my body,' she said wryly.

'Travel by boat,' he advised, indicating the hotel launches and the long motorised canoes in the bay. 'I suggest you go back that way when you fly home. It's cheap—and a lot quicker. When are you going home?' he asked smoothly.

'It depends,' she said, her eyes shining with joy. 'It could be in two weeks, or never. It's up to fate and what happens when I meet your father.' And there was no way that she could keep the eagerness out of her voice.

Pascal nodded slowly as though he already knew some details of her visit. 'And whether you can bear the boredom of such isolation,' he said softly.

Mandy looked around and sighed. 'I wouldn't get bored. I love remote places,' she said warmly. 'I live in a tiny little village in Devon and I hate crowds.'

His heavy lids half closed over the deep blue eyes. 'You *like* isolation?' he asked, as though that was a failing on her part.

Puzzled, she explained. 'I prefer living in the country but I do enjoy company. I'd be quite happy stuck in the middle of a forest, providing I had someone to talk to.'

Pascal let out a long breath. 'My father doesn't entertain. He has few friends.'

Mandy looked at him in surprise. 'Some people like their own company,' she remarked politely, wondering why he'd confided that piece of information to her.

'Life with him would be very lonely,' he said flatly.

'Y-y-yes,' she said hesitantly. 'But he's got you, hasn't he?' she added with a gentle smile.

'Like your villa?' he shot at her suddenly.

Her smile broadened. 'It's wonderful, like a luxurious tree-house,' she enthused warmly. 'I've been treated like a princess. Champagne in the fridge, a basket of weird fruit, garlands of flowers over every available surface—even around the bath taps! How's that for a welcome?'

'Warm,' agreed Pascal in his honeyed drawl. 'Bordering on the enthusiastic.'

'It's fantastic. I'm walking on air,' Mandy confessed. 'I can't thank your father enough for organising it so beautifully.'

The chiselled lips thinned. 'You will. I'm sure he'll get his pound of flesh,' Pascal murmured enigmatically.

Mandy looked at him with anxious eyes. Did he mean that the solicitor's fees were excessive? Still, presumably whoever had hired Pascal's father could afford the cost—or maybe they wanted to find her so much that they'd pay anything to get her. A soft affection filled her eyes.

'I know he'll expect fair payment,' she said dreamily. 'That's reasonable since we could both be benefiting from this. You don't get something for nothing, do you? For instance, I imagine that even the view from my villa must be costed in the overall price.'

'What a practical turn of mind!' he murmured. 'What view do you have?' he asked casually. 'Which one have they given you?'

She thought of it with such pleasure that she wanted to share it with him. 'Up there,' she said, pointing at the gazebo poised some way up the hill, above the circular reception building. It was just visible amid a tumble of purple and red. 'I have this incredible open-air deck—I swear it's larger than my whole house put together! And it's smothered in bougainvillea and I look down on banana trees and coconut palms with little yellow birds flitting around—'

'Bananaquits,' he supplied with a languid air—but watching her intently.

'Bananaquits!' she repeated in delight. 'And the black birds like starlings on stilts?'

'Grackles.'

Mandy laughed—a gurgling chuckle that welled up from her great happiness. But, instead of smiling back at her as people usually did, Pascal remained neutral, as though he found her joy a little childish. She didn't care. If she was unsophisticated, so be it. Right at this moment she could have hugged everyone in sight.

'I'm going to buy some biscuits to feed the birds,' she said contentedly. 'They're amazingly tame. I think I'll spend quite a bit of my time on my deck. The view is stunning. I look across that valley to the hill,' she said, waving expansively at the jungle. 'I can see the ocean and the two mountains—Herbert, the minibus driver, said they were volcanic cones or something—'

'The Pitons,' provided Pascal lazily, his eyes as sharp as glinting knives.

'Yes,' she said, in a voice tinged with awe. 'Aren't they something? Two triangles—just like the mountains that kids draw! Herbert lives near them—can you imagine having that view every morning? We had a long chat. He showed me his family photos,' she added softly, her eyes glowing at the memory of the man's friendliness.

'Herbert got chatty with you?' he asked in a tone of mild surprise. *'Herbert?'*

'Yes. Do you know him? I love talking to people, don't you?'

Pascal lifted a hand and rubbed the nape of his neck thoughtfully, his brows angling to meet in a frown over his nose. 'He's wary of strangers.'

Mandy laughed again. 'But you can't sit next to someone for an hour and a half and remain strangers! I'm going to visit his family some time. Won't that be lovely?'

'Lovely,' Pascal said faintly.

'Oh,' she said, remembering, 'if that fits in with your father's schedule, that is,' she amended.

'Do what you like.' He paused, his mouth set in lines of barely concealed triumph. 'Your time's your own. He's ill.'

'Ill!' The news brought her up sharp. 'Oh, dear. Poor man.'

Pascal's sky-blue eyes seemed to cloud briefly and then his expression became sunny again. Sunny...with clouds imminent, she thought apprehensively, because there was a reserve about the man's manner which she couldn't quite understand. And why the triumph?

'He's quite sick,' he drawled with a mystifying relish.

'I see,' she said slowly. 'What a shame! I was so looking forward to meeting him today.' She put a hand to her head because it was still buzzing from the effects of the journey and she couldn't think clearly. 'I'm awfully sorry,' she said sympathetically.

'How kind. I'll tell him. You look a little tired. You'd better sit down,' Pascal said soothingly, taking her arm. 'Come right under here, next to me. You'll burn that tender skin if you don't take proper cover. You don't want to go home red-raw, do you?'

'Er...no.' Uncertainly she allowed herself to be drawn down to the soft, warm sand.

'Drink?' he asked politely, shifting into the full glare of the sun so that she could take all the shade.

'Thanks. I'd love one. Something fruity and cold, please.'

'Certainly. Simon will be along in a while, I expect.'

The worries were crowding back into her mind. 'How ill?' she asked anxiously, slipping off her shoes and wriggling her bare pink toes.

He gave the scuffed, much repaired condition of her shoes a detailed scrutiny and then looked sideways to meet her troubled gaze. 'Too ill for you,' he said softly.

She frowned. Either her imagination was running riot or he'd just been rude. 'I am very sorry to hear that,' she said sincerely, ignoring his lapse. 'Anything serious?'

'There's always hope,' Pascal said with a grave expression.

'That ill?' Mandy soberly sifted sand through her toes. 'It sounds as if he won't be able to see me for a while,' she said a little tremulously.

'If at all,' agreed Pascal placidly.

'No!' Her hand fluttered to her mouth, his words throwing her into total confusion. And then she put aside her own needs and thought of the poor man, fighting some dreadful illness. 'That's terrible!' she exclaimed in sympathy.

'Isn't it?' Pascal's eyes filled with silvery lights. 'Father will be deeply touched by your concern.'

She bristled at the slicing edge of sarcasm. 'I meant what I said,' she said huffily. 'You think I'm mouthing platitudes, but of course I'm sorry! I feel sympathy for anyone who's ill.'

Pascal's gold-tipped lashes swept down to veil his eyes. 'How nice. Life has made my cynical.'

'That's a shame.' But suddenly she wasn't thinking about Pascal at all—or even his father. Her own troubles were looming too large. 'It's left me with a bit of a problem,' she said slowly. 'My air ticket has to be used by the eighteenth of February. That's less than two weeks away. And your father only paid for my accommodation at Anse La Verdure till that date. What shall I do? I can't possibly afford to stay any longer—'

'Shame,' he echoed insincerely.

Mandy stiffened and flushed at his mocking tone. He wasn't exactly being helpful. Quite at a loss, she stared at the sand between them, watching a tiny crab laboriously hauling itself out of a hole and dumping a clawful of sand onto a small heap at the entrance. She sighed, identifying with the crab's efforts. She'd been fighting

her way out of holes for years. She looked closer. Or
was the crab *digging* that hole for itself to shelter from
the burning sun?

She lifted appealing eyes to Pascal's amused face. 'I
don't know what to do,' she confided.

'Have that drink,' he suggested, either unaware of her
distress or completely indifferent to it. A brief lift of his
hand in the air seemed sufficient to bring Simon running,
the young man's bare feet kicking up small flurries of
sand as he hurried over.

There was an exchange of friendly conversation in the
strange local patois she'd heard several times already,
before Simon went off convulsed with laughter at some
teasing remark. For a moment Pascal looked rather
nice—the sort of man she could confide in, who'd share
a laugh and be jolly when life became tough—and she
was glad that he wasn't too cynical to be nice to Simon.

Emboldened, she reached out and touched his arm.
'You will help me, won't you?' she said persuasively.

'Of course,' he said smoothly, giving the lie to the
message in his frosty blue eyes. 'I'll give you the best
advice I can,' he assured her.

'Please do!' she said fervently. 'I've no idea how to
proceed.'

The lips smiled, the eyes didn't. 'I think,' he said, with
a regretful sigh, 'that all you can do under the circumstances is to enjoy your holiday here at my father's
expense, go home on the eighteenth, and hope that he'll
arrange for you to come over again some time in the
future.' He creaked the smile a little further but the
dimples didn't appear.

Her pulses hammered like small drums. He wanted to
get rid of her, she felt sure. But why? Trying to be gen-
erous, she decided that she might be posing a problem
under the circumstances. It was more than likely that
his father had left a backlog of work at his office. She

knew from her days as an office worker that difficulties
arose when a key member of staff was ill.

Maybe Pascal was involved in trying to lighten the load
for his father's firm—and she was just another problem
that they wanted to shelve for the time being. There might
be more pressing cases to deal with...like defending those
clients charged with crimes, she thought vaguely. But
her case was important too! No one knew how desperately she needed Pascal's father. It was only fair to make
that clear.

'You're right. What you suggest would be the sensible
thing to do,' she agreed reasonably, startled by the
genuine and delighted grin that lit Pascal's face. She
smiled back ruefully, knowing that she'd blow his hopes
of clearing her file from the in-tray. 'However...and I
can guess that this won't be what you want...' she said
sympathetically, 'I'm afraid I couldn't possibly do what
you suggest. I have to stay, somehow.'

He gave her a sharp look. 'Why?' he asked tightly.

She smiled gently at his determination to protect his
father from extra worry. 'I'm too close to my dream.
To walk away from it, to risk losing the chance I've been
given, fills me with horror. I can't give up on this.'

'You'd be wasting your time,' said Pascal coldly.

She noticed that the tiny pile of sand between them
was much larger now. The crab had laboriously exca-
vated a home for itself, grain by grain. It seemed like an
omen and she gave a sigh of satisfaction.

'I don't think so. Your father may be my saviour,' she
said huskily. 'When I knew what he might be offering,
I was over the moon. It's everything I've always wanted.
To be honest, I'd have surfed across the Atlantic to come
here, knowing what might transpire! I appreciate that
you won't understand what this means to me—'

'On the contrary, I do.' Pascal impatiently swept a
hand through the mass of silky gold hair that haloed his
head. 'In my time I've seen plenty of women like you

passing my father's way,' he said shortly. 'Bright-eyed, hungry, hoping their lives will be radically changed.'

She beamed in delight. From what Pascal was saying it seemed that his father specialised in missing-person or lost-daughter cases. 'Your father's quite a guy,' she said in admiration.

'His reputation on the island is second to none,' agreed Pascal cynically.

Mandy decided that if Monsieur St Honoré had such a good track record there was all the more reason for her to stay. She clasped her hands together tightly, her hopes rekindled.

'If you have had experience of women like me before, then you'll know how desperate I am,' she said, her face impassioned as she strove to engage Pascal's emotions. 'I *have* to hang around here. I've got to wait till your father's better. He can make my life perfect.' She smiled dreamily. 'It would be a new kind of life entirely. With someone for me to love, someone to love me...'

'My God!' he muttered.

She flinched, but she lifted her chin, determined not to be crushed by his look of revulsion at her sentimentality. Love wasn't nauseating and Pascal was missing a lot if he thought it was.

'I know I'm hoping for a lot—'

'Dream on,' he said scathingly.

'I will,' she said firmly. 'And my dreams will come true. I am a romantic, but I don't apologise for that. I don't care what you think—what anyone thinks!' she added, defending her beliefs. 'Ever since I saw your father's advert I've been so excited—dancing on air, half-scared, half-thrilled. And I don't care who knows it. It's been a long time since I've felt so happy.'

He grunted, unmoved by her happiness. 'Pity you're going to be disappointed.' And Pascal lay back on the sand and closed his eyes in dismissal. 'He won't be well enough to see you before the eighteenth.'

Mandy frowned with irritation. He was being difficult. 'In that case I'll have to get a job,' she said, with more conviction than she felt.

'You won't be able to,' he muttered irritably, not even bothering to open his eyes and talk to her properly. 'You'll never get a work permit. Jobs go to St Lucians. So, if you haven't any funds, how do you think you'll manage?'

Mandy didn't waver. She'd shift the ground from under him even if it meant doing it grain by grain! She grinned at the image and felt a bit better. 'Well, do me a favour and save me from selling my body in the open market-place,' she said jokingly. 'I'm sure you can help me if you put your mind to it.'

His eyes opened and pinned her with a baleful look. 'Are you suggesting I finance you myself?' he asked coldly.

'No!' She checked her exasperation. 'Look, your father must have someone who's deputising for him now he's ill. Couldn't I talk to that person? I appreciate you must have a thousand and one things to do and I don't want to be a nuisance, so if you'd just tell me where his office is I'll go there in the morning and make my own arrangements,' she finished briskly.

'That could be difficult. He doesn't have an office.' He smirked at her surprise.

'Well, wherever your father usually sees his clients,' she persisted sweetly, wondering why he was being so obstructive.

'In bed?' murmured Pascal, lifting a wicked eyebrow.

Her eyes flickered. 'Yes, in bed! Why not?' she countered pleasantly, calling his bluff. What a ridiculous remark to make!

Pascal let his gaze drift insolently over her body and she wished that she hadn't made the joke. It was perfectly obvious that he was thinking lustful thoughts because his eyes had become drowsy and his expression

was smouldering. Surely he *must* have realised that she
was being sarcastic?

'You come to the point with astonishing bluntness.
The very idea fills me with horror. I think we can try to
ensure your relationship never gets that far,' he said
levelly.

She heard the threat that edged his voice and read the
message in his eyes. Goose-bumps rose on her arms. He
was totally hostile to her. Why?

'Your sense of humour's deserted you! And so have
your manners. You ought to be helping me,' she said
impatiently. 'If your father should learn how—'

'Don't threaten me!' he snapped. 'You're not seeing
him, so get that into your head!'

His hostility was out in the open now. Mandy fumed.
'There's no need to be rude!' she said stiffly. 'Arrange
a meeting with one of your father's colleagues for me.
I'm sure you've been asked to give me what help you
can—'

Pascal interrupted her with a disparaging snort. 'Yes!
Unfortunately for you, however,' he said coldly, 'I'd
rather help a snake find a vein in my leg than do anything that would assist either you or him.'

'What?' she gasped.

'You're on your own,' he growled. 'Don't expect anything from me. To be frank, Mrs Cook, if I had my way
I'd feed the two of you a hefty dose of rat poison.'

CHAPTER TWO

MANDY gaped like a floundering fish. 'I don't know why you're being so insulting!' she cried in astonishment. 'You talk as though you hate your father, and that's your prerogative—but how—why—can you hate me? Why are you being so unpleasant? Is it because my clothes are cheap and out of fashion and I can't afford decent shoes?' she suggested, stung by his look of contempt. 'Because I don't wear make-up or go to a swish hairdresser?'

'I don't care what you wear—' he began.

'Then why keep staring at me?'

He seemed surprised, as if that was news to him. And then he drew in an irritated breath. 'I despise you because of what you *do*,' he growled. 'Dammit! I need a drink. Where the hell is Simon?' He scanned the far end of the beach.

Mandy was silent for a moment, a frown jerking her dark brows together. He knew about her work, then. What was wrong with being a postmistress?

She saw that Pascal was looking at her hands, which had been unconsciously plucking at the hem of her dress and screwing it into a rag—a certain give-away of her chaotic feelings. Miserably she smoothed the crumpled cotton over her exposed white thighs and clasped her hands firmly in her lap.

'Look, I do my job to the best of my ability.' That seemed to make his mouth curl even more. Baffled, she sighed and gave up. 'Think what you like,' she said impatiently. 'I'm determined to wait for your father—if

29

only to commiserate with him! Poor man! I hope I never
have a son like you—'

'The very thought makes me go cold!' he bit out.

Mandy was struck dumb by his savage reaction.
'Something's bugging you! Tell me what it is!' she
demanded.

'Are you that insensitive that you don't know? You're
the problem. You and my father!' he snarled, his teeth
almost tearing at the words. 'Be in no doubt as to how
I feel. I hold my father and you in contempt. I refuse
to lie down and let him grind his heel in my neck! I will
not help women who want to use him for their own mer-
cenary means! Got that?'

She drew in her breath. Their eyes met, glacial blue
and startled brown. 'The message is crystal-clear,' she
said with icy dignity. 'When your father recovers—'

'Maybe he won't,' Pascal said with soft savagery, as
if he wasn't particularly concerned.

He carried his hatred like a spear, thrusting it at anyone
who was associated with his despised father. Pascal's
hostility was worrying her. The bitterness between him
and his father ran very, very deep. There was an anger
in Pascal that was greater than anything she'd known
before. And she wondered what had happened between
the two men to make them such implacable enemies.

A feeling of dread crept over her. Pascal saw her as
an ally of his father's. Not only would Pascal refuse to
co-operate, but she'd bet her bottom dollar that he'd do
his best to stop her mission out of pure spite.

'You can't take your anger out on me—it's un-
reasonable!' she complained. But nothing moved in his
face. No pity, no softening of that twisted, stony mouth.
'I'm sorry you think of your father as your enemy. It's
terrible.' And it was a dreadful waste. She'd have given
anything to have a father. 'But what's the point of revenge? It will only hurt you both,' she argued.

'I'm not looking for revenge,' he said tightly. 'I'm looking for justice. Don't interfere in my life. Don't offer advice and smother me with your sweet, sentimental idea of close family ties! You know nothing of what's going on!'

'No, I don't. It's obviously something immensely important to you. I'm sorry,' she conceded with contrition.

Pascal looked strained. 'Yes. You should be. Now you know the score. Enjoy your holiday and then go home.'

'I can't do that,' she said quietly. 'I'm sorry you won't help me but it doesn't make any difference to my decision. I have to see him.' And she set her mouth in firm lines.

'I'll stop you. Come hell or high water, I'll keep you two apart.'

His voice was quiet but utterly determined and Mandy felt a quiver of alarm run through her body. The circumstances which had put father and son at loggerheads must be more serious and far-reaching than she could imagine. Something terrible had happened between them that caused the bleakness in Pascal's cold blue eyes and the tensing of every muscle in his body to straining point whenever he referred to his father.

'There's more to this than I know, isn't there?' she said.

Pascal nodded. 'Much more. You don't want to get caught up in it. Do the sensible thing. It's in your own interest not to stay.'

Feeling defeated, Mandy miserably picked up her shoes and stood up in a liquid flow of limbs and body. 'I'm sorry you're both so unhappy,' she said, feeling sad for Pascal and his father, and he gave her an odd, suspicious look. 'I'll make my own enquiries. People here will know where your father is—'

'They don't,' he said coldly. 'He's in a private hospital. Strictly no visitors. No calls.'

She heaved a sigh. 'Then I won't disturb him. You said he didn't have an office but he must have a colleague who can help me—'

'A colleague?' Pascal said scathingly. 'He doesn't have one.'

Mandy drew in an exasperated breath. 'Then I'll ring the solicitor in London,' she said, beginning to lose patience. 'Mr Lacey will give me a contact address—'

'Don't waste your time asking,' said Pascal. 'He's had strict instructions not to reveal any information whatsoever. Only to give you the airline tickets and the accommodation voucher.'

'How do you know?' she asked suspiciously.

He gave a small smile of triumph. 'I saw the instructions to Lacey when I was sorting through my father's papers.'

'I see. Well, it doesn't matter,' she said, bravely stopping her lower lip from wobbling. Somehow she needed to see those papers. Pascal wouldn't help, but maybe someone else would. 'I've come so far, I can't give up now! I can still ask around. People are always willing to talk to me. I'll find out. I've spent half my life battling against the odds. Finding your father won't be any problem for me, and I'm sure he'll see me when he feels a bit better. I can be very persuasive.'

'With a body like that, I'm sure you can,' he commented insolently.

Her eyes flared in astonished affront but she forced herself not to dignify his insult with a reaction. Furious with him, she turned haughtily on her heel and walked to the shoreline, determined to prove that she felt so full of confidence that a mid-afternoon paddle was the only thing uppermost in her mind now.

In fact, she needed time to think. Tired from travelling all day, shaky from Pascal's awful reception, she was finding it hard to pull her woozy brain together. The earlier elation had vanished, leaving a heavy depression, and she'd need to overcome that if she was to make any headway with her plans.

As she walked through the cooling water with her head held high to catch the light breeze on her hot face, she wanted to cry because she felt quite weak with disappointment. This had begun with such promise!

She was tired of struggling. She wanted Dave back. Strong arms to hold her. Someone who cared, who'd give her support and encouragement. The world was a lonely place when you had no one, and she'd been alone for too long.

The tears threatened to spill out and she blinked rapidly in case Pascal could see her face and would think that she was upset because of him. She didn't want to give him that satisfaction. What a brute he was!

She'd almost reached the rocks at the end of the beach when a hand gripped her shoulder. And she flinched because it was so similar to Dave's—similar but different. Harder. Less loving, less gentle, more masterful and compelling. Pascal.

'Oh, why are you following me?' she asked in despair.

'You need persuading,' he said curtly.

'I *won't* be persuaded! Get lost!' she snapped over her shoulder, almost at the end of her tether.

Abruptly, she found herself being pivoted around like a doll. They stood very close in the rolling surf and the drag of the water was so strong that she kept losing her balance as the sand was sucked from under her feet.

'Careful.'

Pascal steadied her, his hands sliding to her arms. Irrationally, she longed for him to hold her closer and say sorry, he'd help. And then she'd cry the tears she'd been holding back in sheer relief.

'I don't need you!' she muttered, more for her own benefit than his.

'You will always need men,' he observed, a husky warmth threading his voice. 'Need them, want them, encourage them.'

She blinked in surprise and turned her head away to gather her composure. He was horribly right—not about the encouragement, but yes, to be totally honest, she did need them, want them.

Dave's death had rendered the thought of loving another man inconceivable. But certain things—lovers kissing in a bus shelter, passionate scenes on the television, and personal memories of making love on a warm, moonlit night with the curtains fluttering in the soft breeze—all these and more had repeatedly jolted her deep sexuality into life again, driving her crazy with the torment, brutally reminding her how wonderful married love could be. And she hungered for something she could no longer have, because she'd never fall in love again and sex without love—without marriage—was unthinkable.

She missed being hugged by her beloved husband. She missed the joy of sex. And the bliss afterwards.

Slowly her limpid gaze came back to focus on his. 'Spoken like a true chauvinist,' she said resentfully. Yet the memories had roughened her voice and she sounded horribly husky and inviting.

'You need men ... and I need women. There's something terrible about the sex urge, isn't there, Mandy?'

Taking advantage of her astonished silence, he slowly displayed his masculine approval by openly studying her body. Mandy squirmed uncomfortably, aware that her sweat was holding her thin dress against her damp skin and that he must be learning more about her figure than he should.

'Don't!' she husked, reeling from his intense sexuality. It was making her body throb... It was such a long time since a man had been so bold and poured desire from the depths of his eyes! Her mouth trembled and pouted. 'Don't!'

'Invitation and rebuke. Little-girl sweetness, womanly sensuality. Demure and innocent, yet offering the promise of curves that will fire an old man's loins. What a joy you must be to lustful old satyrs,' mused Pascal with breathtaking insolence.

'*What?*' she gasped.

'Easy arousal is vitally important when you're dealing with lowered libido,' he drawled.

'Is that an observation from personal experience?' she snapped waspishly.

He smiled with the confidence of a man who knew he couldn't ever give the impression that he might be less than one hundred per cent pure male. 'I have a very high libido. It's a problem sometimes,' he murmured. 'Particularly when faced with temptation.'

Her chin jerked down, following the direction of his fascinated and mocking gaze. The freshening breeze— or *something*—had teased each dark centre of her breasts into a firm peak which thrust at the cloth assertively in an unspoken invitation. No wonder Pascal's mouth was looking sultrier by the minute! Hastily, she covered their come-and-get-me appeal with defensively folded arms.

'Don't flatter yourself that that's anything to do with you!' she snapped. 'Get your libido back in line. I'm not interested in you—'

'What about money?' he suggested.

'All I'm interested in at present is your father—'

'They amount to the same thing. He represents money for you.'

'He represents my dreams,' she corrected.

'You're determined to stay on, aren't you?' he murmured. 'So...we'll have to get along together after all.' His mouth twisted at her wide-eyed hope. 'Would you like to spend an hour or two on my boat?' he suggested casually.

Although he was smiling at her innocently, she couldn't mistake the sinfully arched eyebrow and the undercurrent of male desire in his deep blue eyes.

'No. I wouldn't. And I know what you're suggesting and you're no gentleman—'

'True,' he admitted. 'I'm the local rogue.' And he flashed his dazzling, tigerish grin.

She was beginning to get his measure. A playboy. Rolling in his father's hard-earned wealth.

Perhaps, she thought, elaborating on the theme, the antipathy between father and son came from Monsieur St Honoré's resentment at having built up a thriving legal practice only to have his son lounge about on beaches, chat up women and spend his money.

'You've made that perfectly clear by your clumsy invitation,' she said coldly, deciding to scramble over the rocks to the next bay and escape his unwanted attentions.

'Good. Because I don't want you to think I'd ever play fair,' he told her silkily, and she paused, wondering what he meant. Her hesitation gave him the opportunity to capture her wrists in his vice-like hands. 'You and your kind are like parasites. And, for your information, I invited you to my boat on the off chance that I could keep you there till you promised to get the hell off the island,' he added, with no shame at all for his attempt to manipulate her.

'If you don't take your hands off me,' she said coldly, 'I'm going to scream. And I can scream for England, I promise you.'

'Surely you don't want any publicity?' he murmured. 'Not the kind of woman you are.'

She tried to speak, but her throat was filled by a hard, dry lump. What kind of woman did he mean? she wanted to ask, horrified to be thought anything but hardworking, moral and conscientious. But the curl of Pascal's lip, the flinty scorn in his piercing eyes and the intensely physical threat of his muscular body made her feel as if she'd committed an indecent act and ought to be hiding herself in shame.

Dawning on her slowly was the realisation that he knew something about her background—something so dreadful that any decent person would be justified in despising her and her kind. What kind? Who *was* she?

Mandy's sharp, shuddering intake of breath sucked in his warmth, the scent of his powerful male body. A shiver skimmed down her back. If she was right, she didn't want to hear the truth from this unsympathetic brute. The revelation should come in private, from someone who might care about her feelings. The shock that there might be awful secrets in her family past had shaken her to the core. She wanted to know *now*. Or she'd have a sleepless night filled with the sound of her own sobbing.

Sound suddenly forced its way through her white, trembling lips. 'Pascal,' she said rawly, 'I pray that somewhere inside that steel skin of yours is a heart. Because I need to find it.' Her hand reached out in an urgent plea because she knew she had nothing to lose. 'I beg you, take pity on me—'

'Go home. Staying here will destroy you,' he said grimly.

She winced. 'I *have* to stay! You *know* why I'm here!' she cried, looking up at him through swimming eyes. 'Don't you feel any compassion for me?'

'Not a scrap.'

'Forget your bitterness!' she begged. 'Forget whatever vendetta lies between you and your father! I *badly* need to see him; you must realise that! I can, I *will* do it the hard way if I have to, but you can make it a lot easier and save me time. Whatever your feelings, please, in the name of humanity, arrange a meeting for me as soon as he's better! I've come all this way, my hopes raised...'

Her voice trailed into silence. He had moved even closer, so that her fingers touched his chest. Blinking, she registered the firm, moulded muscle, the warmth and the flawless texture of his skin that cried out to be stroked. Beautiful, she thought, much to her own surprise, and had to fight against the foolish, knee-jerk urge to slide each palm up to his gleaming brown shoulders and hold him close, because the lure of that warm body was overwhelming.

She pulled herself together. 'Please,' she repeated, her hazel eyes huge with anxiety and her whole heart in her long, pleading look.

'You were right. You can be very persuasive,' he said huskily.

'Oh!' she breathed, filled with hope. 'Pascal...' Her voice dried up.

Serious and unnervingly determined, he slowly reached out with his forefinger, and Mandy watched it come closer to her mouth, knowing that her lips were parting and that her breath was rushing from her lungs in a long, low sigh. Hunger. Hunger for a man's touch!

She stopped breathing, fighting her need for comfort and love. It had happened once before, when she'd been desperately lonely and in need of affection. A million hormones had flooded her brain and made her behave stupidly, allowing an acquaintance to kiss and caress her and touch her body till she'd found herself hating the fact that he wasn't her late husband. And she'd spent the next twenty minutes fighting and coaxing and pleading to be left alone.

She recognised that her body still yearned for a lover. But not this man. So, to save herself, she whipped her head around and the fingertip briefly touched her teeth, then slid across her jaw and throat before it was retracted.

But she couldn't erase the memory of his burning blue eyes spilling desire into hers, or the faintly salty taste of his finger and its erotic, tantalising caress that promised much, leaving her suffering from a sense of emptiness. And she knew that she was out of her league and that the few men she'd known before had been relatively unsophisticated and inexperienced compared with the knowing Pascal.

She and Dave had been like happy children—sweethearts for a long time, marrying young, loving, playing, laughing. After he'd died men had tried to make headway with her but her heart and body had been frozen in time...

The sea lost its sparkle and grew dim. Dim because tears were filling her eyes. Crying! And Dave had been gone for two whole years!

Why did she feel so emotional? Was it the long journey? Was it the joy of finding herself in a tropical paradise and then the let-down when the promised meeting with Vincente St Honoré had failed to materialise? She groaned softly. Perhaps it was because she feared that her hopes might be cruelly dashed. Or perhaps it was the anticlimax from the high tension and excitement of wondering if she might at last be on the brink of tracing her true parents.

And now, to top it all, there was the all-pervading fear that her family hid a dark and alarming secret.

Pascal must be aware that she was crying. But he remained still and silent. Her cheeks grew wet and salty tears reached the corner of her mouth because she couldn't rid herself of the despair.

She licked them up, lapping them with the tip of her pink tongue while she reflected that she wanted to find her parents more than anything in the world. It had always been in her mind, even though she'd been happy in the children's home because Dave was there, and Dave had been first her childhood friend and then the man she'd wanted to marry. He'd become her husband immediately she'd left the home on her eighteenth birthday, and their bliss together had more than fulfilled one of her dreams.

Her other dream was to know if her mother was still alive and who she was. And she'd also dreamed of helping her mother if necessary—because she was sure her mother wouldn't have abandoned her at the Glasgow nursing home unless she'd been desperate.

Mandy knew that she needed someone of her own to love. Dave's death had left an emptiness that had grown worse with time, not better.

I'm terribly alone, she thought, her lower lip stubbornly refusing to stop quivering. I want to find my roots, whatever they are, and I'm close, very close, but fate in the shape of Pascal St Honoré is stopping me—

'My father would adore you,' said Pascal softly, touching her wet cheek.

'That's nice,' she husked shakily.

'No, it's not.' A big, solid hand came to rest on her slender back and she felt herself shudder. 'It's the last thing I want,' he said tightly.

Slowly she turned her head to look at him and, though he must have seen the tear-stains on her unhappy face, his bleak and anguished expression didn't change. There was disapproval set like concrete in his expressive mouth. Not one ounce of compassion.

His gaze slid away. 'Simon's on his way with our drinks from the beach bar at last. Wipe your eyes,' he ordered.

Pride was enough to have her surreptitiously wiping her tear-stained face with her handkerchief, thankful that Simon had a long way to come still and that she'd be halfway decent by the time he arrived.

She felt worried. There must be a reason why Pascal felt such disgust for her. For the first time she questioned the wisdom of seeking her roots. Maybe the cost would be too great and the anguish of knowing the truth could hurt her badly.

'I need your help,' she said in a low voice.

'You have serious doubts now, don't you?' murmured Pascal soothingly. 'You're beginning to see that it might be unwise to pursue your goal.'

'Yes,' she agreed.

'Good. Very good,' he approved.

He gave her a long, slow look that seemed to heat her very soul. Something was crackling across the space between them—an electricity, a wave of male energy that poured through her lowered defences and seared directly into the secret places of her body. Her lips parted, her breath shortened in dizzying confusion. Muscles tightened in spasms in that core deep inside her that only Dave had ever liquefied before.

'Pascal, I—' she began doubtfully.

'Act normally,' he muttered in an undertone. 'Wait till Simon's gone and then I'll tell you what I'm prepared to do for you.'

The words trembled with a warmth that seemed to slip through every vein in her body. And she wasn't sure what he meant, only that he was going to help.

'Thank you,' she breathed gratefully.

Pascal's golden brow winged upwards, his voice still rich with sensuality. 'You'll thank me more thoroughly than that before I'm through with you,' he promised.

His meaning was now plain. Mandy's eyes widened in shock. 'You're shameless!' she said indignantly.

'With a father like mine, it's inevitable,' he drawled. 'Drink, lady?'

Mandy looked up at the young St Lucian, bestowed a shaky smile on him and accepted the exotically decorated glass of juice. It would give her something to do with her hands. Right now she felt an overwhelming urge to slap Pascal's smug face.

'Thanks, Simon. I needed this,' she said with heartfelt gratitude, and took several long sips through the straw. 'It's very good,' she said, trying to take her mind off the hovering Pascal. 'Lots of spices.'

'I'm sorry it took so long,' Simon said to them both. 'One of us was up at the main bar getting more ice and I was trying to catch a dog running loose on the beach. I brought a refill for you both, in apology.'

'I can certainly drink them both. I'm so hot. Wait a minute. I can finish this one now... There.' She exchanged the empty glass for the full one, a little worried that her body was definitely not acclimatising to the sun. Suddenly she felt quite heady. 'I'm sorry you've had to come all this way,' she said with a warm smile.

The young man grinned at her, slid two tumblers of amber liquid from the tray and handed each one to Pascal. 'No problem. Signature, please,' he said, handing a receipt book to Mandy.

Pascal and Simon indulged in another round of friendly banter while she went over to a rock and settled herself down on it with her feet in the surf. The white, frothy juice slipped down her parched throat and eased her tension at once. Was there rum in it? It was difficult to tell, it tasted so spicy.

'What's in this?' she asked suspiciously.

'Papaya, mango, sour-sop, cinnamon, ginger, cumin,' Pascal replied. She nodded. The warming spices. No wonder her body glowed. 'What do you know about my father?' he shot at her suddenly, catching her unawares. 'Do you know he's a lecher and a liar?'

She stared wide-eyed at his expressionless blue eyes and felt a deep sympathy. Hating your father might actually be even worse than growing up without one. At least if you were ignorant of your father's character you could pretend that he was everything you would have wished for. She shivered as a tremor of dread iced her spine. Maybe she would do better to remain ignorant of her own parents.

'I know nothing about him. Whatever the truth, I'm very sorry for you both because you hate him,' she said earnestly, swishing her hot feet in the cooling water.

Languidly she tipped back her head. She ought to find some shade soon. The sun's glare was very fierce and it was making her a little dizzy, so she brought her head level again.

Pascal flicked away the sticky drops of water that had condensed around the bottom of his empty glass which he'd been resting against his chest. He placed the glass on a rocky ledge behind him and picked up his second drink.

'If you like,' he suggested, 'I will give you a free ride on my boat to the airport when your two weeks are up. I must strongly advise you never to make any attempt to see my father, however tempting the idea might seem. You would almost certainly regret it.'

Mandy felt her heart beating faster. His threat had scared her. Giving him the benefit of the doubt, she decided that maybe he was being kind and trying to keep her from being hurt by discovering the secret of her family. She shook her head to clear it. 'I need time to think,' she said slowly.

It was difficult. Her brain seemed addled. For the life of her, she could think of no other logical reason why Pascal should warn her. Unless it was somehow to his advantage.

Advantage... That popped a memory into her head: the wording of the cryptic advertisement. 'Please contact the office below where you will learn something to your advantage.' She pursed her lips. His father had placed that advert and he'd virtually promised her something good. Her eyes shone. Something good! *Not* bad. Not frightening or disgusting!

Either he or Pascal was lying. But which of them?

'Decided?' he asked silkily.

'No.' She moistened her mouth with another long sip of juice, closed her heavy eyes and let the sun warm her lids. She was getting tired. The journey had sapped her strength and she wanted to lie down and rest, but she couldn't let Pascal see that she felt weak to her very bones.

Her eyes seemed reluctant to open. Slowly her lashes lifted, fluttering with the effort. The sun and sea were so dazzling to her eyes that they were blurred. As though through a fog, a thought surfaced in her mind.

'You were looking through his papers.' She frowned, finding it difficult to formulate words, and wondered if she was suffering from jet lag. One of the people whom she delivered mail to had said that it only happened on west-east journeys, but he could have been wrong. 'What did you dis-discover about me?' she asked carefully.

'Enough,' he answered curtly, draining his glass. He shot her an assessing look. 'Enough to damn you.'

She stiffened, her eyes rounding in distress. She couldn't form the question in her mind. And maybe she would be wise never to ask, never to know. 'You—you're frightening me,' she managed at last.

The fierce blue eyes burned with a cold, piercing fire. 'So I should hope. The whole thing alarms me,' he said softly.

'No!' she moaned. All her instincts were telling her to run from the truth, to leave the island and let her past remain a secret known only to Pascal, his father, and...her relative. The person who had paid to have her brought out to St Lucia.

'You can't stay. Your life would be a living hell,' persisted Pascal remorselessly.

She gave a shuddering sob, seeing ahead of her her slow coming to terms with being quite alone in the world, never to find her family.

She gulped, emotion and weariness making it hard for her to get her words out coherently. 'Tell your father I w-wish him well and I'm...sorry to let him down. I hope he feels better soon,' she added, trying to hold her fuzzy mind together. 'Poor, poor man.'

Something dark and anguished flickered in Pascal's
eyes and then his lids dropped to conceal whatever secrets
lay there. 'Poor man, hell! Last time I saw him he was
screaming abuse at the stretcher-bearers,' he said quietly.
His mouth twisted at the memory and when he saw her
sympathetic expression he lowered his lids again to
conceal anything that might betray his true thoughts. 'I
gather from your sweet, parting sorrow that you've decided to call it a day.'

'I *think* so,' she said slowly.

He swung her limp body around to face him and
Mandy's dulled brain registered the shaking in his hands
that betrayed an extreme tension. 'Stop *thinking*. Just
make sure you go. I don't want to see you hurt,' he said
softly. 'And if you stay you will be, I swear. Do the
sensible thing. Get a suntan, eat, drink and be merry
for the next two weeks, then leave St Lucia and don't
ever come back.'

She tried to focus on what was going on all around
them and to see herself enjoying a holiday at Anse La
Verdure. Carefully, elaborately, she built up the picture.

People were having fun. Scuba-divers were out on the
coral reefs, people were snorkelling a few yards from
where they sat. 'It looks nice,' she mumbled.

'It's wonderful. See the catamarans cruising by?' he
said persuasively. 'Holiday-makers come from the north
of the island to gape at the Pitons, which you have on
your own doorstep. Look at the elegance of the yachts
mooring in the bay. This is such a perfect place to anchor
and the water is so clear that people sail from other
islands to dive and swim, to eat in the beach bar or the
restaurant complex above the beach. And you have it
on a plate. Free.'

She passed a sweaty hand over her hot forehead. All
along the beach the sunbathers slept, tanned and caught
up with their holiday reading. Even to her confused mind
she could see that it was a beautiful hide-away and totally

peaceful in the absence of any traffic. The dominant sound was that of birds, singing in the forest that began where the sand stopped.

Mandy closed her eyes, imagining herself on the homeward journey. She would be alone, still with a huge question in her life unanswered. But this time it would be worse than before. There would be a bigger question mark hanging over her—not just the identity of her parents but what they had done. And how that affected her.

And then she knew that she had to discover everything there was to know about her background; every nightmare had to be exposed. Because, if she didn't, she'd have those nightmares anyway—every single horror that could be imagined. If she was ever to know herself, she needed to know the truth.

White-faced, she began to gather all her courage, all the strength and dogged determination that had stood her in such good stead over the difficult years in the past. Without a doubt, she'd need every ounce.

CHAPTER THREE

SLOWLY Mandy opened her eyes and a wave of nausea hit her. Grimly she fought it down, realising to her dismay that her stomach had been so churned up with the unfolding nightmare that she was feeling quite ill, just when she needed to be strong enough to take whatever came her way.

Pressing a hand to her middle, she tried her best to calm herself with some long, deep breaths. But they made her dizzy and nauseous again and she slanted an alarmed glance at the watchful Pascal. 'I don't feel too good,' she said miserably. 'I need to lie down.'

Her free hand drifted vaguely over her forehead and found beads of perspiration there. It was the heat. She needed fluids. Her drink was still in her right hand and she gulped it down fast, draining the glass. Then she stood up to go and sat down almost immediately. Something hot and fiery was coursing through her stomach and her legs had melted along with every muscle in her body.

It was more than sunstroke or the spices in the drink. Closer to flu, she thought woozily. Or some virulent stomach bug—already! She let out a little moan to bewail her bad luck.

'We'll get you to your villa,' came Pascal's voice, a million miles away. It seemed almost concerned. But she must have been mistaken, because she thought he said, 'And I'll give you ten thousand dollars to get out of my hair and off the island *now*.'

'Ten thousand?' she repeated uncertainly.

'You're not asking for more, are you?'

The world went fuzzy. She looked down to quell the nausea, and the waves lapping her feet became a blur. When she laboriously lifted her head to judge his meaning, she found that his strong, dark face was hazy too, and her mind wasn't connecting properly with her body. Or her mouth.

'How could it be...enough...when I could have...?' she began, shaping the words painstakingly and feeling worried about her woolly tongue. Food poisoning, perhaps. Something on the plane...the ice in the drink... 'I want—' She blinked. He was peeling her fingers from the glass and removing it from her hands. 'What...was I s-saying?' she asked, stumbling over the sentence.

'That you want to accept my offer of money to go immediately,' he replied silkily.

'No! I wasn't! Why are you offering me money?' She frowned over the way her mouth had become all lips and tongue and how carefully she had to concentrate on her words. 'Ten thousand won't buy me—'

'That's the price,' he said shortly. 'Take it or leave it.'

She couldn't have moved if she'd tried. Her body had turned to stone. The waves slurped backwards and forwards over her ankles, backwards and forwards with a dizzying effect... Afraid that she'd lose her balance, she pressed her hands firmly into the jagged contours of the rock and concentrated hard.

'I'll l-leave it. I want—'

'To go home,' he supplied helpfully. 'I'll take you to your villa and get your things together while you lie down. I doubt you can walk straight—'

Mandy's eyes rounded. He could be right. Through the fog she saw that he'd lifted an amused eyebrow, mocking her confusion. And then she realised what he'd done.

'There *was* alcohol in that fruit j-juice, wasn't there?' she said in dismay. 'I wasn't sure...I thought there might be, but—'

She broke off in mid-sentence because he was smiling. And she knew that she'd knocked back—what?—three strong, alcoholic drinks in an alarmingly short space of time!

As she swayed Pascal placed his arm around her waist and laughed softly, the warmth of his laugh floating over her parted lips and making them feel in dire need of a kiss. Startled, she blinked, but was mesmerised by the swimming depth of his sea-blue eyes, his too near mouth, the even white teeth in the deeply tanned face.

'Voodoo Punch,' he murmured in her ear. Her inhibitions had been loosened from their tight control. His warm breath made her tremble as it teased her skin. He gave a slow and self-assured smile. 'Your drinks contained a hefty slug of rum. One Voodoo Punch can be invigorating. Two tend to remove constraints. And,' he said in a 'don't blame me' tone of voice, 'you had a Planter's Punch in the bar when you arrived. Unwise in this heat.'

'I asked you for fruit juice!' she wailed indignantly.

'Something fruity,' he corrected.

She groaned and worried over the thin line between the effects of alcohol and sexual desire, because there was a lovely warmth heating her pelvis and her breasts, a deep warmth that flushed through her body like the aftermath of love. No wonder people drank! she thought faintly.

'The rum was disguised!' she muttered crossly, her hand drifting up so that it could hold her head in one place. 'I knocked it back too fast. Don't you know how dangerous that could have been?' she asked in a rush of anger.

'Not for you, apparently,' he said, totally unconcerned. 'I took the precaution of asking Simon if you'd had the "welcome" drink. He said you tossed it down as if you were used to it.' He grinned at her with his hungry tiger's grin. 'The rum did wonders to the way you walked down those steps and across the beach.'

He'd seen her then? The warm air seemed to wrap itself around them both, intensifying the huskiness of his voice, the steadiness of his compelling gaze. 'What way I walked?' she asked uncertainly, her mouth working hard on shaping each word properly.

'As if your muscles had been loosened by sex, by love, by alcohol. It's not a very English way of moving,' he explained. 'More fluid and Tahitian. Very sultry and exotic. Erotic. Every male on the beach was fascinated.' There was a purr to his voice and it curled into her with a deep intimacy that made her feel uncomfortable. And vulnerable.

His fingers lightly stroked her shoulder and she felt the pressure from each firm pad burn into her skin. But still she couldn't move. It was all she could do not to slump disgracefully to the sand in a helpless heap.

'Punch-drunk!' she groaned, annoyed at his amused chuckle. 'And I thought I was getting in the holiday mood...and feeling relaxed!' She struggled to overcome the lassitude. Tentatively she stood up. Sea and sky hurtled around in a wild loop-the-loop, and sand and sunbathers described a kaleidoscope of colour. 'I feel dreadful!' she muttered.

'You look it,' he agreed, brutally frank. 'But incredibly sexy.'

A sun-heated arm came around her. But she jerked away from his embrace because only Dave had ever held her that close and no man was going to poach on his territory.

'Don't *touch* me!' she seethed. 'How *could* you do this to me? It's so humiliating. I want to lie down! Find me a sun-lounger in the shade and leave me in peace!'

Ignoring her wishes, Pascal drew her back into his arms with a quiet laugh. Unfortunately, her body was too uncoordinated to reject him again. 'Everywhere in the shade has been taken,' he crooned. 'With skin as pale as milk, you'd get second-degree burns if you fell asleep in the sun. I'll get you to your villa.'

Her villa. The last place she should go with Pascal accompanying her... She took several deep breaths. His skin felt like soft, warm water flowing over rock and her heart had reacted to the discovery by lurching into a reggae beat. Furiously she cleared her head.

'No. Find—find Simon. He can help me—'

'Simon,' he said in amusement, 'would get the sack if he had to handle you the way I need to. Come on. You know it makes sense. We'll pretend I'm a Zimmer frame, shall we?' And with surprising gentleness he gingerly moved her to the dry sand.

Zimmer frames weren't covered in living, breathing, silken skin that vibrated beneath her leaning body. They didn't have muscles that rippled and bulged with power, or hands which spanned the curve of her waist and shifted with every movement, giving her an expert and disturbingly enjoyable massage.

Her mind was wandering. She had to get a grip. They had a fair distance to cover. Miles. Well, several hundred yards, dotted with thatched shelters and reclining bodies and hazards like palm trees to dodge.

'I can't! People will see I'm tipsy!' she wailed, and blushed at the very thought of facing the disapproving stares during every future mealtime.

'Not if we cuddle and pretend to be lovers,' soothed Pascal.

Mandy groaned at the very idea. 'You think that's better?' she squeaked. 'You think I could l-let them believe that you'd picked m-me up on my first afternoon here, and that we've got to the cuddling s-stage already?' But she knew she didn't have any option.

'You have to let them think you're drunk *or* affectionate. Take your choice,' he answered smugly. 'I'll let you stagger over on your own if you like.'

'Brute!' she mumbled, grabbing her shoes and trying to aim them at her wet, sandy feet. 'Oh, get in!' she ordered her toes, grabbing at Pascal when she almost toppled over.

He chuckled and hauled her close against his body, both arms wrapped around her. 'If two legs won't hold you steady,' he said in amusement, 'what makes you think you can manage on one?'

'Optim...optim... *Hope*,' she muttered, wriggling away with dreadful reluctance and trying to get a wayward toe into the canvas shoe. But her mind—what there was of it—had been fatally diverted; assailed by his physical presence, by the clean scent of his hair, the salty taste of his shoulder where her protesting mouth had briefly passed.

So he crouched down on his haunches, keeping one hand in contact with her body, allowing it to trail in a lightning movement over her breast and waist before it curved around her trembling thigh.

'Oh!' She shuddered with involuntary desire.

'My sentiments exactly,' he said huskily. He lifted his lashes and gave her a smouldering look and Mandy realised to her dismay that she'd spoken aloud, and wanted to groan some more to release the backlog of breath that seemed to be building up in her chest.

Gently he removed her shoe and began to dust the sand from her toes as well as he could. His touch was delicate and careful, belying the potential strength of his big hands. And there was something achingly sexual about his concentration, the curve of his lashes on his fine cheekbones, the slight jut of his upper lip. Each small toe was tenderly brushed free from sand and he checked her shoes before persuading her feet to slip inside. She felt cherished, and tingled right through all the sensation-hungry parts of her body and up to her brainless head.

All the while she wobbled outwardly and inwardly too, and despairingly placed both hands on his tousled curls so that she didn't disgrace herself by collapsing. The sun had turned his hair into liquid gold. His curls shone as if they'd been filled with light and flipped up at the nape of his neck. And, in the haze of the late afternoon and the haze of her mind, she felt an uncontrollable urge to let her fingers thread through the shimmering coils and gently draw him up, turning his strong-boned face to hers so that she could release her emotions in a fierce kiss.

Instead she stood—she hoped—as stiff and as unresponsive as a block of wood. The alcohol was eating her brain! she thought miserably, when the moment was over. Hope and disappointment, apprehension and setbacks had all combined to heave her emotions into the melting pot.

Pascal managed to slide his way up her body as he straightened and she glared, wishing that she could risk stepping back and thereby avoid the invasion by his searching hands.

'Ready to go?' he asked. She nodded sullenly and he gave her a charming smile. He was apparently in his element because he was *in* charge and *in*dispensable, she thought crossly. 'Put your arm around my waist,' he said cheerfully.

They began to walk to the steps. And she hoped that most people would be too engrossed in their paperbacks to notice that she and Pascal were wrapped so enthusiastically around each other.

'You've made a fool of me!' she muttered.

'Thank you,' he answered gravely, as though she'd complimented him. 'I've had enough practice. My father's always luring beautiful women and I'm always getting rid of them.'

'Thank heavens I'm not beautiful,' she said, trying to work out what he was driving at.

'No, you're not,' he agreed equably. 'Not conventionally so. But you're sexy and you have a certain gut appeal and that's what men want.'

Mandy shot him a scathing look. As she and Pascal crossed the sand to the dreaded steps she hoped that he'd been lying about his father. She didn't want to deal with a lecherous solicitor whose behaviour was even worse than his rakish son's.

'Climbing boots on?' Pascal asked cheerfully when they reached the foot of the steps.

'Mount Everest!' she said wryly, glad that he was giving her a breather. She was certain that her feeble legs wouldn't get her to the top.

'Funny how booze and sex have exactly the same effect on one's leg muscles, isn't it?' commented Pascal loudly, just as a couple of American women passed them.

The women gave a joint intake of breath. Mandy briefly closed her eyes. 'Don't!' she pleaded. 'Please don't shame me any more! I wish I'd never seen the advert that brought me here!'

'It would have saved me a lot of hassle if you hadn't,' Pascal agreed quietly.

And she knew that the regret in his low tones was genuine. For some reason he felt that he had to keep her from his father. It was such a driving need, in fact, that he'd offered her a huge sum of money as a bribe. There was something odd about that. What would he gain?

'Let's go.'

She resisted. 'I can't *think* if I'm moving—'

'I know. Quick. Before too many people see you.'

The idea appalled her, as, no doubt, he'd planned. She postponed the thinking and kept her mind fixed on reaching sanctuary. As if to hasten the moment when he could get rid of her, he drove her upwards, all but lifting her from step to step at a breathless pace.

Several people passed them, all smiling sentimentally at what must have looked like two lovers—perhaps a honeymoon couple, she thought with dismay—snuggling up together on their way to their villa. And she felt worse and worse the higher they climbed, because her soggy leg muscles ached from the unaccustomed exercise and Pascal's hold became bolder and more possessive.

'Just a minute,' she whispered, leaning helplessly into his body because her legs refused to take her any further.

'You're so defenceless. It's deeply attractive,' he murmured. And he took advantage of her listlessness, his hands smoothing down her back towards her hips.

She jerked away. 'You need locking up!' she ground out in temper.

'I've been locked up!' he said tightly. 'So don't push me too far. I'm not the kind of guy who lets others walk all over him.'

She began to shake. 'L-locked up?' she stuttered.

'Prison.'

Mandy tensed every muscle and remained utterly still. 'What for?' she breathed.

'Criminal damage and actual bodily harm.'

Mandy screwed up her courage despite his forbidding expression. 'Why?' she asked harshly.

He hesitated, as if debating the pros and cons of telling her. His face seemed suddenly all angular bone, as if the skin had been drawn into a tight mask. But the lines around his strained mouth and the desolation in his silvered eyes spoke volumes. Her heart tumbled over and over. This was the cause of the pain, the root of the anger he carried inside him, and she waited, wide-eyed, for him to speak, because she wanted to know what was driving him to his extreme behaviour.

To her disappointment Pascal slowly shook his head. 'I don't see the point of telling you, if you're going.'

'Tell me,' she demanded.

And apparently he couldn't resist her round-eyed appeal, because he shrugged and said, 'I attacked my father. He'd been careless with one of his cigars.' There was a long pause which she didn't interrupt. Pascal's mouth thinned. 'He threw it away in my garden and burnt my house down. My—' His next words were cut short when he clamped his mouth shut.

Mandy's face softened in sympathy. The loss of his house and possessions had obviously affected him deeply. She wanted to say something but the words wouldn't come, though he must have seen her concern because his eyes softened for a moment before they were concealed by his lowered lashes.

'That's all you need to know,' he said. Mandy knew that there was something else that caused him to look so haunted and wished he'd confide in her. Most people did. Pascal was more controlled. 'Just don't push me too far, Mandy. I might do something we'd both regret. I don't want to hurt you,' he said gruffly. 'I would like us to come to an amicable agreement. But if you're difficult there might be trouble. Understand?'

'Yes,' she agreed. Amicable. That was all she wanted. She was too tired to put up any kind of fight.

Then he was propelling her up the steps again. She was so absorbed in wondering what else had happened that she stumbled, grazing her ankle slightly on the rough volcanic rock.

'Mandy! Are you all right?' Pascal's exclamation of genuine concern made her even more confused than ever.

'It's nothing,' she answered hastily as his troubled blue eyes met hers. 'I'll face worse, perhaps, when I get to meet your father.'

He froze and then quickly brought her around to face him, the kindness wiped from his face. 'You said you were going home!' he said sharply.

'No. *You* said,' she corrected. His mouth tightened and she looked at him warily. 'What are you going to do now?'

'Whatever I have to,' he said grimly.

It was an empty threat. He couldn't do much, she thought; they'd finally reached the restaurant and reception building. Mercifully, plenty of people could see them because it was an open-sided affair, poised halfway up the hill below the individual guest villas. In the bar and lounge above the restaurant waitresses were serving tea and cakes and shooing away the tropical birds which flew in from the flame-flowered trees.

Not far now and she'd be shot of him. One of the staff would help her from here. She could crawl into bed with a couple of aspirin and a wet towel for her head. 'I can manage now,' she said stiffly, trying to sound capable.

'I think not.' Pascal stopped, his weight holding her back, and he waved a greeting at the waitresses with his free hand. '*Bonjour*, Lucretia, Shelly, Cynthia!'

Mandy stiffened. He was attracting the attention of every waitress in turn! There were six of them, all dressed in white broderie anglaise tops and the traditional pastel tartan fabric that Simon had called madras. They politely greeted Pascal and nodded at her. Silently she suffered their stares and slight air of shock. Their disapproval stemmed from the fact that she was being hugged to Pascal's hip like a Siamese twin.

'You beast!' she muttered, rounding on Pascal. 'They must all know I'm a new arrival—'

'And they'll think you're a quick worker,' he pointed out, before coversing in patois with one of the women.

She could pick out a couple of French words—she'd become quite fluent whilst working in a Channel ferry office a number of years ago—but everything else rendered his words annoyingly incomprehensible. Mandy felt like sinking through the floor.

Her brain fired warnings at her to abandon him here, now, in full view of the women, before her reputation suffered any more. But she felt exhausted after the long climb in the sultry heat.

'Let's move on,' Pascal suggested finally, sounding pleased with himself. 'I think they've formed their opinions of you.'

She clenched her teeth and resisted. An idea had occurred to her. 'Not yet. I n-need a longer breather before we go on up the hill,' she whined, deliberately sounding pathetic.

Pascal was, as she expected, quite content to give everyone in the bar more time to see their intimacy. 'Suits me,' he said expansively.

It suited her too. She searched her mind for the name of the tall waitress who was cutting slices of cake at the bar. 'Agnes!' she called plaintively. With a dramatic gesture, Mandy pressed a fluttering hand to her forehead and willed her tongue to behave. 'Would you have anything for a sick headache?' she asked hopefully.

'You feelin' sick?' exclaimed Agnes, coming over to them with an expression of obvious relief.

'Very,' said Mandy truthfully. 'Monsieur St Honoré has very kindly helped me up the steps. My head's spinning,' she said, allowing her body to tremble, just as it wanted to. 'I feel awfully hot and dizzy.'

'I can see you're shaking! Just you wait there a moment,' said Agnes, putting a sympathetic hand on Mandy's arm. 'Hold her good, Monsieur St Honoré,' she added politely. 'I got something for her.' And the concerned Agnes bustled off in a flurry of broderie anglaise and madras.

'Clever,' murmured Pascal, his mouth tight with annoyance.

'Thanks,' she said gratefully to Agnes, who'd appeared with a glass of water and a pop-strip of two pain-relievers. Mandy flung Pascal a look of triumph from under her lashes.

'You need any help, Monsieur St Honoré?' asked Agnes in a remote tone.

'Yes, please!' cried Mandy quickly.

'No!' He gave Agnes a disarming smile. 'You're busy. I can manage. Mrs Cook doesn't want any fuss.'

'Sure you'll be all right?' Agnes asked Mandy with an anxious expression.

Mandy swallowed the two pills and returned the glass. She felt awful and she had a hurdle or two to get over before she could feel really safe. 'I'll be fine when I can lie down,' she said shakily. 'Monsieur St Honoré can see me to my door—and then,' she added, brightening at a sudden inspiration, 'I'd like him to stop here on his way back in a moment or two and accept tea at my expense, as a thank-you.'

Agnes nodded. Pascal launched into a long stream of patois and she went off to the bar.

'What did you say to her?' asked Mandy suspiciously as Pascal began to help her up the hill towards the canti-levered villas, looking out over the jungle.

'That I'd be with you for an hour or so. And that I'd like her to ring the boat and let them know it might be a while before I'm back,' he said blandly.

'You'll leave me at my door,' she muttered crossly. 'I need to be alone! I can't stand having you around any more!'

The walk up the hill was longer than she remembered. She plodded on, trying to think of nothing at all.

'Almost there.' Pascal's accent was more pro-nounced, the Caribbean drawl more languid and seductive.

Her head was spinning with it. 'Fine. Leave me now!' she demanded weakly.

Pascal gave a short laugh and abandoned her, totally, as she'd asked. Surprised, she sat down suddenly on a nearby wall. She needed him! The awful truth made her break into sobs. She'd had enough. Life had thrown too much at her and she couldn't cope.

'Stubborn woman,' sighed Pascal, and swept her up into his arms, carrying her the last twenty yards along the hibiscus-lined path to her door. Refusing to listen to her whimpering protests, he turned her key in the lock, walked across the tiled hallway to the open deck and gently arranged her on the tartan madras settee.

'That'll do,' she whispered miserably. 'Go!' He disappeared from her immediate view. There were odd sounds coming from her bedroom, but she couldn't raise the effort to lift herself from the deep, plump cushions and see what he was doing. 'Go away!' she yelled in exasperation.

'I'm fixing your mosquito net,' he called back.

Mandy sighed and gloomily watched the humming-birds busily extracting nectar from the bougainvillea. Gradually her tears ceased as she became lulled into a false calm by the glorious view. The two mountain peaks rearing into the cobalt-blue sky, the tropical hillside and the sparkling sea would have mollified anyone.

It was breathtakingly beautiful. She was lucky. And, awful though she felt, she was on an island in the West Indies, poised—perhaps—to learn something to her 'advantage'. Once she'd scraped Pascal from under her feet.

With a calmer mind she found that her logic returned. Slowly she reasoned that it was quite likely that there was nothing unpleasant in her background at all.

He'd been trying to get rid of her for reasons of his own—reasons to do with his terrible rage against his father. Perhaps when Pascal knew that she really was determined to stay he'd come clean and tell her why he was so hell-bent on getting her off the island. And she was curious to know what else his father had done to drive Pascal to such violence. Something extraordinary, she was sure. Her hands trembled a little as she contemplated her meeting with Vincente St Honoré. And she hoped that he wasn't as evil as Pascal had suggested.

But, however worried she was, she had to solve the mystery surrounding Vincente's client. His—or her—identity intrigued her. The hotel was so exotic and obviously expensive that she knew her summons must have been financed by someone important. That might be her mother or her father—or even a rich relative. Whoever it was, he or she must be on tenterhooks, wondering if the solicitor had made contact yet.

It dawned on her that it might be someone who didn't dare reveal the existence of a love-child—someone with a family already, in a position of trust and responsibility.

She was impatient to know the truth. She'd find out, she thought sleepily, and yawned.

'It must be bedtime in England,' Pascal said idly, parking himself on the deck near her feet. 'How do you feel?'

'Fine,' she lied, turning her green-flecked eyes on him.

'Then I'll leave,' he said surprisingly, 'when I've cleaned this graze.'

She felt the gentle dab of soft cotton wool on her ankle and was too weary to remonstrate. Carefully he cleaned the broken skin and patted it dry, applying a little cream he'd found in her first-aid kit. His expression was absorbed and deceptively tender and she wished that he were really kind and not just hanging around and killing time, hoping everyone would think that they'd been making love.

'That'll do!' she said resentfully. 'You've stayed long enough.'

'As you like. Will you go down for dinner?' he added with polite interest.

All she wanted was the oblivion of sleep and a snack—and to be alone. 'I'll get room service,' she said warily. 'That way the staff will be able to see for themselves that you haven't stayed the night.'

He nodded and stood up. 'So they will. Sleep well.'

Before she could move, he'd bent his head and pressed his lips to hers in a long, deeply satisfying kiss that had her longing for more. But he merely stared deeply into her treacherously wistful eyes, lightly trailed his fingers down the side of her face, and strode out. Leaving her nonplussed.

'Oh, hell and darnation!' she breathed.

She'd been so close to reaching up for him. She *had* to find her family and channel her affection or she'd be in serious trouble! So much love to give, no one there to receive it. Perhaps she ought to adopt a kitten, she thought gloomily.

She didn't feel inclined to move a muscle. All the stuffing seemed to have been knocked out of her body. For a long time she lay on the settee while the peace of the lush valley descended on her mind, creating an oasis of calm till she finally struggled to her feet. It might have been nearly six o'clock local time with the sun beginning to set, but her body told her that it was five hours later. Pascal had been right. It was bedtime.

After loosening her hair and taking a shower to freshen herself up and clear her headache, she lifted the gauzy net that hung from a central point above the bed, and, because she felt so hot, slipped naked into the comfortable, king-size bed. It was wonderfully romantic to be surrounded by a muslin tent; to feel so warm that she could dispense with a sheet and lie with the moonlight silvering her pale, gleaming skin.

The massive louvred doors that formed one wall of her bedroom had been folded right back so that the room was open to the air. From where she lay she could see across the wide deck to the tops of the banana trees with their huge, paddle-shaped leaves, and the small yellow birds, hopping around the coconuts clustered in the gently clacking palms. Bananaquits. Lovely, she thought muzzily.

In the morning she'd begin to unfold the mystery of her summons to this beautiful island. Maybe she'd discover the truth about the St Honoré men too. But her priority, she thought dreamily, was to know that she wasn't alone in the world. And with that hope in her heart she promptly fell asleep.

CHAPTER FOUR

IT MUST have been hours before Mandy woke, because she felt almost refreshed. It was warm, deliciously warm, and the air on her body caressed it like a lover's breath.

'Mmm...' she sighed, and stretched slowly and thoroughly with her eyes tightly shut like an indulged cat, her back arching from the bed while her hands drifted upwards over the surface of her silken skin in pure hedonistic pleasure.

In private if nowhere else she could indulge in her love of sensuality—rare but much adored treats of perfumed baths, satin wines, dark, dark chocolates. For a while the ache in her heart could be alleviated. Her senses could be placated. It wasn't the same as being loved, but preferable to sensual starvation.

Languidly her arms lifted above her head to scoop the heavy weight of hair from her neck before allowing it to fan out across the pillows like the waves of a dark sea.

Lost in the world of uninhibited eroticism that lay between sleeping and waking, she inhaled the perfumes in her nostrils; strange scents—steamy soil, exotic flowers, the pure Caribbean air drifting in through the open doors which led to the deck.

And, feeling extraordinarily relaxed and serene, she let her ribcage rise and fall with each long, slow intake of breath, and listened in delight to the deafening sound of torrential rain battering the huge leaves of the banana trees which draped over her balcony.

The rain stopped suddenly as if it had been turned off at the mains, leaving another sound to dominate. Her eyes snapped open and, to her surprise, it was still dark—a thick, velvet darkness like a warm cloak. The unusual sound intensified and she eased herself up onto her elbows, tilting her head to listen more clearly to the noises in the jungle outside, like—

'Tree frogs,' supplied a soft male voice.

Mandy screamed in shock. She dived for the top sheet, which lay tangled in a heap at her feet, while simultaneously darting nervous glances through her heavily tumbled hair at the shadowy figure in a chair by the bed.

'Who—who are you?' she husked nervously. 'What . . . are you doing here?'

'Waiting.'

Waiting! She trembled. All she could make out was a pair of gleaming eyes, flashing white teeth and a white dinner jacket. But the strongly accented voice had been Pascal's. The shoulders were his. The sheer *nerve* was his.

And she was naked. It was dark, she told herself, tugging at the stubbornly muddled sheet. He couldn't see her properly. But already her eyes were getting accustomed to the murk and she could see every one of her toenails with alarming clarity.

She gulped, getting redder and redder as she fought the stubborn tangle of material and tried to keep strategic parts of herself adequately covered at the same time.

'Oh, drat the wretched thing!' she fumed in panic.

'Shall I help?' he offered politely.

'No!' she yelled as he half rose from the chair. 'Stay away! Don't come near me! How the devil did you get in?' she demanded angrily. An end. She'd found the end! Now where . . . ?

'The door. I left the key in it,' he admitted absently, as though his mind was on something else.

It was: the spilling flesh of her breasts, billowing from her totally inadequate hand and arm. She doubled over and shot him a filthy look which he missed entirely because his gaze was raking over her slender back and the long curve of her hip and thigh, and she groaned because heat was skimming the surface of her skin where his eyes lingered. It was like being licked by fire.

'Wretched sheet!' she muttered, taking her temper out on it.

'I suggest a technique similar to the fan dance,' he said, watching her struggle for dignity with open amusement. 'The skill lies in releasing one fan while covering yourself with—'

'Turn away!' she demanded furiously, trying the method. If she folded herself forwards, she could ease the sheet up without revealing anything vital...

'Not much point,' said Pascal in a low, liquid drawl. And she could *feel* the interest in his voice as she clumsily completed the manoeuvre, every bone in her spine tingling from his fascinated gaze. 'I've been here for hours.'

Mandy choked and jerked her head around in horror. 'You...you sat there and...*watched*?'

'Not much else to do. I couldn't read,' he said reasonably. 'It was dark.'

'You—you voyeur!' she spat.

'Oh, no,' he assured her disarmingly. 'Not my style at all. I prefer to take an active part.'

'Active!' she breathed, hastily hauling yards of linen around her as a defence against 'active'.

'Uh-huh.'

She felt the breath clog up in her tubes. The tree frogs whirred on, oblivious to her dilemma; the perfumes of the night drifted in, filling her senses. If she hadn't been wrapped up like an Egyptian mummy—with a carefully tucked-in mosquito net to contend with too—she would have legged it.

Mandy licked her lips nervously. The darkness was too intimate, the setting too romantic. She'd felt like a fairy-tale princess when she'd gone to sleep, a sensual woman when she'd woken, but now was a vulnerable innocent on the point of disenchantment.

'Put the light on!' she ordered sharply.

He rose from the chair, stretching his legs with a quick frown at their stiffness, and went over to the light switch, giving it a cursory flick. Nothing happened. 'Storm's affected the electrics,' he said, unruffled. 'It happens every now and then. I'll light the candles.'

'Candles!' she groaned.

She'd noticed them when she'd gone to bed and had thought then, How romantic. Romantic she didn't want. From under her gauze tent Mandy watched Pascal light the first one, his absorbed face flickering with shadows as he slipped the glass shield over the flame. Warily she watched him walk around the bed and strike a match for the second.

Transfixed by the set of his sensual mouth, she gave an involuntary quiver. Any woman would be quivering if she had been woken by Pascal, she thought in excuse. He was very handsome. Especially in a dinner jacket. Now that both candles were alight, the floor-to-ceiling mirrors behind the bed reflected the soft light—and the magnificent cut of Pascal's jacket. Or perhaps it was the magnificent chest that filled it.

And to her eyes he looked more rakish than ever, partly because his black bow-tie had been undone and was hanging loosely around his neck while the collar of his dress shirt exposed his bare throat, and partly because his jaw and upper lip bore the dark shadow of a burgeoning beard and moustache. Designer stubble, she decided scathingly, though she had to admit that it was wickedly attractive. She imagined he knew that and wished she didn't. Something dreadful had happened to her inhibitions.

'Now you can go,' she said coldly, flicking her tumbling hair back decisively.

'Not yet.' He sat down again, crossing his elegantly clad legs.

Mandy shrank warily back against the pillows, her naked shoulders golden in the soft light. 'So you think you're going to seduce me?' she challenged bluntly, saying it before he did.

'As if!' he protested, with the air of a shocked monk.

'Oh! Then...why—why come here? Why...?' She licked her lips in embarrassment. Why watch me? was a stupid question. The answer was perfectly obvious.

'You think that the only reason I might be here is for sex?' he enquired with an air of faint reproof.

Mandy glared through the curtain of silky dark hair that had flopped over one eye again. Yes! she wanted to snap, sensitive to the hot, humming space between them. 'You could be sleepwalking, I suppose,' she said tartly. 'Or lost. Or—'

'Concerned,' he suggested with a bland smile.

'Judging by your previous performance, that's unlikely!' she scathed.

He lifted a golden eyebrow in disagreement. 'I got you back here, didn't I? I stopped you from reeling drunkenly across the beach.'

She glared. 'Yes! But you got me tipsy in the first place!'

'I might have encouraged you to have a drink but I didn't pour the stuff down your throat,' he pointed out. 'You did. And I was worried. You didn't order room service—I checked. You hadn't changed your mind and come down for dinner, because I was in the restaurant and would have seen you.' He leaned forward, nothing but friendly enquiry on his face. 'I came to see if you were all right.'

That seemed out of character. She gave him a disbelieving look. 'I'm fine. And I don't believe a word of your story. You were all for feeding me rat poison earlier,' she reminded him. 'If you only came because you were worried, why didn't you go at once, when you saw that I was breathing?'

'Yes,' he said admiringly, pinning his blue gaze to her shrouded breasts. 'You have quite a rhythmic action there.'

'Oh!' she croaked. He knew every intimate detail of her sleeping body! Not only her breasts, but... Thinking of Pascal's fascinated eyes on her casually sprawled legs and the sinfully languid way she'd stretched when she woke made her vocal cords freeze.

Her body was private! she thought angrily. Only for Dave and no other man. And now Pascal had violated her privacy and taken away something she'd shared with her husband alone.

'You rat!' she whispered, tormented by shame.

He leaned closer still, his head slightly angled as if he was puzzled by her reaction. 'Is this modesty? I didn't think it would worry you that much,' he mused, a frown dipping his brows.

Utterly lost for words, she stared back at him and tried to comprehend the kind of life he must lead if he thought women would be so blasé about their bodies—especially if viewed by virtual strangers when asleep.

'Get out!' she rasped. And then she screamed it like a banshee. 'Get out! Get out!' she yelled, every inch of her quivering with helpless rage.

'Please!' He winced. 'Stop screaming for England and listen to me. Other than checking to see if you were all right, I did have another reason for coming into your room—'

'I knew it!' she spat, angrily scraping her hair back again because it had fallen forward in a misleadingly sensual way and right now she wanted to be as sexually attractive as a bowl of porridge. 'You are a lecherous brute—' she began haughtily.

'For bringing you supper?' he asked, apparently pained by her accusations. 'I thought you'd be hungry.'

She was, she discovered to her surprise. Ravenous. But far too suspicious to be taken in by that excuse. 'I don't believe you! Where is it? I can't see it!' she snapped.

'On the deck. With my compliments.'

Peering out, she could see the shape of a tray on a low table, and her stomach rolled at the thought of food. 'So it is,' she said grudgingly. But how could she be sure that it hadn't been an excuse? 'Why didn't you leave it there, check that I wasn't gasping my last breath,' she said waspishly, 'and make a discreet exit? You *didn't* have to sit and watch while I slept!' she accused, feeling the flow of blood staining her skin as she pictured him taking a leisurely look at her intimate secrets. Her eyes closed as if that would wipe the image out of her mind.

'I thought you ought to be watched,' he said levelly. 'You could have been ill from the effects of sun and alcohol.'

'You seem very clued up about it,' she muttered. 'Is that from personal experience?'

'Yes. My father drinks a lot.'

Her brow furrowed as she wondered apprehensively if that was true. But it didn't alter the fact that Pascal had been arrogant in the extreme. 'I don't believe a word of your explanations,' she declared stubbornly. 'But I'm fine and I'm awake so you've no excuse to stay any longer,' she added, refusing to be grateful to him. Food! She felt her mouth water. 'It's late. Almost...' she lifted her wrist and stared at her watch in surprise, then brought it to her ear to see if it was ticking. 'Three o'clock in the morning?' she cried in astonishment.

'That's about right. However, it's about your breakfast-time in England,' he murmured. 'I knew you'd wake hungry after the time-change, and—'

Her eyes narrowed. 'When did you turn up?' she demanded.

'Just before midnight.' He drew a rueful hand over his jaw and she heard the rasp of stubble. 'Don't worry,' he soothed. 'I used the time profitably. I had some thinking to do. And now I'd like to apologise.'

'What?' Her mouth dropped open in amazement. 'You are apologising—after everything you said? What are you up to, Pascal?'

'Roughly halfway through my rehearsed speech of contrition,' he answered drily. 'Let me explain.' He beamed broadly so that the dimples appeared, and she hardened her heart to his suspicious charm.

'Do,' she said coldly. 'But go easy on the treacly smile.'

He laughed softly. 'You have a right to be angry,' he admitted. 'I've harassed you unfairly. I realised that when I swam back to my boat after leaving you. It must have been a very different welcome from the one you'd expected.' He kept the smile going, even when she snorted in scornful agreement. 'I returned to the main hotel complex and waited in the dining room because I hoped you'd change your mind about room service and turn up for dinner. I wanted to buy you some champagne and make amends. I felt rather bad when you didn't appear.'

'Good,' she muttered unsympathetically.

Pascal's eyes twinkled. 'I'd be mad at me too,' he said disarmingly. 'If it's any consolation, I was awash with guilty feelings and didn't enjoy my meal at all. I pictured you alone up here, feeling ill, far from home, knowing you'd have to struggle to stay here—'

'All that,' agreed Mandy coldly, glad of a chance to make him crawl. And she was still suspicious of his motives. The U-turn seemed a bit too abrupt to be true.

'I know. You must have been worried,' he sympathised.

His whole manner was one of penitence, and it sat incongruously on someone so deeply cynical. 'Don't overdo the gush,' she said drily.

'How can I convince you?' he said earnestly. 'I felt so bad that I knew I'd never get a moment's sleep unless I made you feel better. You know how it is when you have something on your mind and it goes round and round your head,' he said, fixing Mandy with his startling blue eyes.

'Yes,' she acknowledged warily. He was very persuasive. The charm just oozed out of him like juice from a mango.

'Then you understand! I couldn't rest. I came hoping you'd still be awake and I brought the supper as a peace-offering.' He smiled hopefully and, try as she might to resist it, Mandy felt her hostility melting. 'Please accept my apology. I shouldn't have taken my anger out on you. My father's the swine. I'll concentrate all my rage on him and not the people he's involved with,' he said quietly.

'I accept your apology,' she said stiffly. 'But your father's ill. You shouldn't talk about him like that—'

'You haven't taken in anything I've said about him, have you? You think he can give you what you want. I suppose it's not for me to disillusion you.' He hesitated, giving her an odd look. 'It's clear that I'm not going to succeed in dissuading you from seeing him. OK. Go ahead. Don't get hurt, that's all. For God's sake take care. Watch your back.' He grimaced. 'And your front.' And he spun on his heel, striding quickly across the floor to the open doorway and the steps leading to the deck.

'Wait! What on earth do you mean?' she cried, scrambling to her knees in alarm.

Slowly he turned to face her again, standing stiff and unapproachable while the background noise of the tree frogs deepened and intensified till it seemed to be whirring insistently inside her head.

'I can't explain. Not here. Not now,' he said, his voice tight and controlled. He looked so harrowed that she was finally convinced. And she felt certain that he was keeping some vital information from her.

'You warned me not to get hurt. Who by?' she demanded shakily. 'Am I in danger?' Her parents? she thought. A jealous relative? How the mind invented horrors when given the chance! 'Tell me! You can't go without telling me!' she insisted in agitation. 'Put me out of my misery!' she begged.

'I can't. You are determined to stay so all I can say is that you must be careful. Goodbye,' he muttered, and he walked without another word from the bedroom. As he went down the steps the outline of his high, tense shoulders were clear against the dark night sky.

'Stop!' she yelled in exasperation. 'Ten more minutes won't hurt! You've been here half the night, for heaven's sake! Stop, please!'

Rapidly she gathered the sheet up and fumbled with the mosquito net, yanking it loose from where it had been tucked under the mattress. And then she swung her bare legs to the floor and ran out, across the deck to where he had paused in the hallway. Goodbye! He wasn't going to see her again—and he knew things about her life, knew his father's contacts...

'Pascal!' she screamed hysterically. He was at the door of the villa. He didn't turn! 'Don't go. Please don't go!' she sobbed. 'You can't leave it like that!' His shoulders gave a little shrug and he walked out, slamming the door behind him. Stunned, Mandy dashed over and flung the door open again. 'Come back!' she yelled as his figure retreated down the steep path. 'For God's sake come back! I need you! You know I need you!'

He paused and she gave a shuddering sob of relief when he swung around, his guarded expression clear in the illumination from the small lamp above his head. 'Are you sure about this?' he called gruffly.

'Yes! Yes, I'm sure!' she jerked out, trying to keep the sheet in place over her heaving bosom. 'Come back. *Please!*'

Pascal began to walk towards her. She let out a shaky breath and opened the door wide for him. He gave her a long, thoughtful look and strode back into the hall. 'You really are desperate, aren't you?' he said softly, and it seemed as if he was struggling with conflicting emotions.

Mandy nodded and shut the door, incapable of speaking. Already the tears were forming, crowding her eyes like drops of rain in a cloud. And he'd see them soon enough and know how important his father was to her. 'Tell me!' she mumbled miserably.

'All right. I'll see what I can do to help you,' he promised. 'Actually, in an odd way, I was trying to help you before, by giving you a hostile welcome.' He interpreted her look of disbelief and smiled ruefully. 'It's true. I felt that it would be better to put you off than to expose you to the consequences of your arrival,' he admitted in a low tone.

Mandy stiffened, her nerves at screaming point. '*What* consequences?'

'I'm sick of putting women together again,' Pascal growled. 'I decided that this time I ought to be cruel to be kind. I did all I could to persuade you to go home—'

'Plying me with alcohol?' she asked accusingly.

'Not quite. But I took advantage of the state you were in. And I deliberately tried to embarrass you,' he admitted. 'I know, I'm sorry, but I can assure you that I judged that a little unpleasantness now would be preferable to much greater anguish later.'

She gulped, sick with a stomach-churning fear; his words had been so sincerely spoken that she was forced to believe him. It seemed that Pascal's father might be everything he'd claimed. And yet . . . she had to meet the man if she wanted to know why she'd been brought to St Lucia. Her legs suddenly gave way and Pascal strode forward, gathering her in his arms.

'I'm sorry,' she mumbled. 'That's so stupid! I'm usually tough and cheerful,' she assured him shakily, hating anyone to think that she buckled under pressure. 'This—this has devastated me. I'm scared, Pascal, by what you're suggesting! My dream's becoming a nightmare! I had impossibly high hopes and I was so excited and . . . and . . .' She sniffed noisily.

'It's all right,' he soothed, stroking her with his voice and with his warm eyes and smile. His fingers joined in as he touched her quivering mouth with gentle understanding. 'You don't have to worry about anything,' he said huskily, kissing her mouth. 'Not anything at all. I will protect you. No one will hurt you, I promise.'

Totally reassured, Mandy just stood there, letting him kiss her better. Flowering under the warmth of his soft, persuasive mouth, she got better and better with every slowly passing second. He'd help her. She had nothing to fear any more. Pascal was strong and capable, and perhaps he'd take over her case from his father and—

She checked herself, realising that she'd let him kiss her for too long. It was not reassurance any more. It had long since become passion. On both sides. 'Pascal?' she mumbled thickly.

'Mmm?'

Denying herself the intoxicating pleasure of his mouth was quite an effort. She guiltily pushed back the comparison she'd half made with Dave's kisses and slid her hand between their lips. Pascal kissed her fingers with equal tenderness and the sight of his lowered lashes made her heart lurch in erratic little leaps.

'I—I'm all right now,' she lied shakily.

He gave a soft laugh, his eyes gleaming brilliantly. 'I wish I was.' The back of his hand caressed her face and she felt her eyes drooping with the deep sensuality that

that gesture aroused in her. And vaguely she wondered why this man—of all men—should be able to tune into her body with such ease. 'I'm sure you'll understand I'm very tired. I've had no sleep,' he was saying when she hastily attended to him again.

'What?' she asked with a frown.

He smiled at her indulgently. 'What I have to say will take a long time and has to be approached delicately,' he said. 'I was saying that I think I should leave—'

'You can't!' she wailed. 'How will I sleep?'

'Mandy,' he said gently, 'don't tempt me. You're very seductive with your hair dishevelled and your eyes like saucers. I'm not immune to you, and the situation—my concern for you and your vulnerability—is endangering my detachment, let alone your interests.'

He slid his hands into her hair, pushing it back and cradling her head. And she let him; she just stood there, enjoying the feel of his warm fingers splayed out, massaging her scalp, lifting the heavy hanks of hair and letting them drift over her shoulders and back till she tingled all over. 'Your eyes have grown soft and warm,' he murmured, staring deeply at her. 'With flecks of honey-gold and green. Your lips keep parting and inviting me to kiss them and I'm finding it harder and harder to resist.'

'We...' Mandy hastily sought to rid her throat of its alarming huskiness. 'We could talk from a distance,' she suggested, her face serious. 'I could get dressed and—'

His finger touched her lips and it was all she could do to stop herself from taking it into her mouth. Maybe he knew that too, because he withdrew it quickly.

'No,' he said firmly. 'It's late. The wrong time, the wrong place. I know you're disappointed,' he murmured, sounding regretful.

'I am,' she said quietly.

'By the time I'd finished explaining to you, the early shift would be around, sweeping the paths, collecting flowers for the rooms and so on. I'd be seen leaving.'

He pushed a weary hand through his tousled curls. 'And I'd be too bone-tired to think up some excuse. I must go. I need my sleep, Mandy.'

'Oh! Of course. I've been selfish. But when...?' she began anxiously.

He smiled. 'Come to the beach in the morning. Any time you're ready.' He patted her hand. 'And now you ought to eat something. The cold spiced chicken is very good. If you can't sleep any more, go for a walk, have a swim, whatever you like, but enjoy these luxury surroundings and put all your worries away. I know how to solve this situation.'

She let his warm, honeyed tones slide into her fretting brain and felt instantly soothed. Her eyes were trusting as they met his, and her smile deepened when he smiled crookedly back at her.

'That's wonderful, Pascal! I'm glad you came and...thanks. You've made me feel better. Thank you for everything,' she added fervently.

The blue eyes flickered. 'My pleasure,' he murmured.

They both jumped. Someone was knocking on the door! Mandy's eyes rounded in alarm. 'Who could that be?' she whispered under her breath, horrifyingly aware that their voices must have been heard from outside because of the nature of the open-sided deck.

'Mrs Cook! Mrs Cook!' called an agitated voice.

'Damn! It's Arcadia!' muttered Pascal. 'See what she wants.' And he quickly hurried back into the bedroom, out of sight.

Baffled as to why anyone should want her at this hour in the morning, Mandy checked that she looked decent, hitched the sheet a little higher and opened the door. 'What is it?' she asked a little sharply.

'Telephone call,' said the breathless Arcadia. 'For Monsieur St Honoré.' Mandy stared at her blankly and the woman looked uncomfortable. 'I know he's around! I heard you yellin' all the way from the night desk in the reception building,' she said obstinately. 'I know he came up with a tray and never came back—not that I did see. It's *important*, Mrs Cook. His father—'

'All right, Arcadia, I'm coming,' came Pascal's authoritative voice.

Mandy froze, watching in dismay the widening of Arcadia's big brown eyes. She heard Pascal walking down the three tiled steps from the bedroom to the wooden deck. Arcadia would be able to see him from where she stood framed in the hall doorway. Mandy turned, walking stiffly away, knowing that his visit would be common knowledge to the hotel staff in the morning.

She found herself clutching the deck rail as if it might save her from being branded a fallen woman. But it wouldn't and she wanted to scream her innocence, even though she was obviously naked beneath the sheet and Pascal had appeared from her bedroom at this ungodly hour. At least he was fully clothed, apart from the loosened tie and collar! She shuddered. Nausea clutched at her fragile stomach and she leaned her head weakly against the upright rail-post.

'Got to go!' called Pascal urgently. 'Remember. The beach.'

'But—!' She whirled around. He'd gone. Arcadia gave her an old-fashioned look and closed the door.

Miserably Mandy stumbled over to the settee, ignoring the food temptingly spread on the table. Outside she could hear his feet hurrying down the path towards the reception building and she cursed whoever had decided that the villas dotted about the hill would offer a total escape from the stress of normal life and therefore be without telephones.

Absently she picked up a chicken leg. Everything she'd done since arriving had managed to suggest that her morals left much to be desired.

People had seen her chatting to Pascal on the beach, 'cuddling' him, staggering woozily to her villa with him.

He *had* jeopardised her reputation! And now that Arcadia had found them together in the middle of the night no one would believe that she'd felt ill at all.

In their eyes she'd be branded a liar and a loose woman. She bit her lip. How ever could she live that down?

Moodily she munched some of the bean and cashew nut salad. Her reputation had been called into question through no fault of her own—or Pascal's. Or...was that true?

Her fork stayed in mid-air, every scrap of her mind dedicated to thinking back over the last hour, while an unpleasant suspicion hammered rhythmically in her head. Maybe he wasn't so innocent. Maybe he'd intended to cause trouble. The fork clattered to the plate, scattering sweet potato on the floor.

'I'll be darned!' she muttered, her heart thudding loudly in her ears. Could Pascal possibly have made *sure* that people knew he was going up to her villa?

It was obviously known that he'd brought her some supper. The only way back to the beach—and his boat— would be past the night desk at Reception. If he didn't reappear for several hours, then that would be evidence enough that he'd stayed the night.

The phone call about his father could have been a bonus...or a previous arrangement. She frowned, wondering if she was becoming paranoiac. After all, Pascal had almost walked off earlier. In fact, he'd been some way down the path when she'd persuaded him to come back.

Mandy's eyes darkened. That could have been a deliberate set-up too! After all, he'd fed her a tantalising warning and then had calmly said goodbye. He must have *known* she'd need an explanation! All it had taken was a few hints of some secret threat to her and she'd practically begged him on her knees to return! At the top of her voice! And he'd obliged.

Aghast at her own thoughts, she sank into the cushions and stared sightlessly into the velvet night. Another tropical rainstorm began to pound the lush foliage only yards away and she held onto the mean-spirited hope that Pascal would get soaked to the skin on his way back to the boat.

She was almost certain that he'd duped her. He was involved in some complicated plot to ruin her good name. And again the question came; why? What would he gain if she left the island? And what would he achieve by making her out to be a cheap little tramp?

All she could come up with was that somehow he stood to benefit from her family. But would his father have been allowed to act as her solicitor if that was the case?

Picking up the fork, she set it on the tray and thoughtfully finished the candied potato with a spoon. But no more ideas came to her because her mind was dwelling on the fact that she'd find breakfast a terrible ordeal.

Furious with Pascal, she went back to bed in the vain hope that she'd sleep. As she lay there the frogs stopped their loud chorus so suddenly that it was as if they'd been switched off. Birds began to sing long before the sky grew light and she listened to them morosely while slumped against the pillows, trying to think of all the things she could do to trace Pascal's father and, failing that, look for clues to the whereabouts of her relatives.

Behind the dark, angular bulk of the Pitons the sky became a pink glow. It faded rapidly to gold and then turned a fierce blue, as hard and uncompromising as Pascal's eyes.

And finally her purpose was clear. At breakfast she'd behave as if nothing untoward had happened. And she'd make certain that Pascal didn't compromise her when they talked on the beach. She would weigh everything he said and did with the greatest care. If he as much as blinked out of place, she'd walk away and do her own detective work, hard though that would be.

reputation! 'Are you a local man?' she asked, hoping that he might help her later.

'Sure I am! I come from the plantation down the coast. Beau Rivage. That means beautiful shore,' he said in his musical voice. 'And if you're Mrs Cook I gotta take you there.'

Her smile faded. 'I am. But who says?' she asked warily. Speaking to Pascal on a public beach was one thing; going off somewhere unknown to meet him would be stupid.

The Rastafarian dug in his shorts pocket and brought out a business card.

'This is from *Vincente* St Honoré?' Puzzled, she read the address: Beau Rivage Plantation. Someone had scrawled underneath, 'Please come.' 'Who gave you this?' she cried in excitement.

'Jemima. Vincente's maid,' said the man. 'It's Mr Vincente's card,' he added unnecessarily. 'She said I was to bring you right over.'

Hardly daring to believe her luck, Mandy thought for a moment. 'Is Mr Pascal there with Mr Vincente?'

That set the Rastafarian grinning. 'If Vincente knew Mr Pascal was on his land, he'd go for his shotgun!'

Mandy beamed. Pascal had been lying about his father's illness. Vincente was waiting for her at Beau Rivage! She had no compunction about standing Pascal up. Her teeth clenched briefly at the prospect of reprisal but she was too elated to dwell on the unpleasant things in life. At last she was on her way to the solicitor's plantation home.

'Let's go!' she said eagerly, slinging her bag over her shoulder.

Happily she clambered into the heavy dugout and sat in a state of excited terror as the fragile boat sped over the water. It seemed very unstable, especially when it met the choppy seas around the headland, and several times it seemed to leap into the air and drop down with an unnerving smack.

'Beau Rivage!' the Rasta yelled finally, pointing to a beach.

It looked completely deserted. Just the beach and coconut palms which ran back through a valley tucked between scrubby hills. 'Where's the house?' she shouted back as the boat drove full-tilt for the beach.

'Down the road a way. He goin' to meet you, don't you worry.' The Rasta killed the engine and then there was silence.

Mandy felt a deep sense of unease. The road was nothing but a dusty track, the plantation looked unkempt and there was a ruined shack just visible amid a tangle of vegetation. Apprehensively she hooked her bare leg over the side of the canoe and grabbed the man's steadying hand. Wading through the shallows with her shoes around her neck, she searched for some signs of life.

'Am I supposed to wait?' she asked uncertainly. There was no answer. When she spun around, it was to see the Rastafarian pushing the boat off the shelving shore. 'Hey! Don't go!' she yelled apprehensively.

Dropping her bag, she ran into the sea, kicking up a shower of silvery water and whimpering at her own stupidity. Pascal! she thought in a sudden flash of comprehension as the boatman roared away. 'Pascal!' she rasped aloud.

Fists clenched, she stood shin-deep in the ocean, soaked to the skin and trying frantically to quell her alarm and recall the geography of the land between the hotel and Beau Rivage—if that was where they truly were—because she'd have to walk back by the looks of it, and that might take most of the day, judging by the dense undergrowth!

There was the track leading into the valley, of course, though she didn't hold out much hope that it would take her to a house as the Rasta had claimed. Dejectedly she turned back to study it again. And saw Pascal.

He came striding cheerfully towards her, dressed in khaki shorts, a jungle-green shirt open almost to the waist and ancient sneakers. And for a moment she was desperately glad to see him. Just for a moment. It passed quickly, leaving her raging at his deception.

'Paddling?' he asked, a grin on his irritatingly cheerful face.

'Cooling my temper,' she said tightly, wishing that she were wearing more than a bathing costume and shorts. 'You deceived me again!' she accused.

'Want to hear my side of it before you hit me?' he suggested, quite unconcerned.

She drew in a deep lungful of air. 'Amaze me.'

'I think I will. Shall we go into the shade or do you want to stay in the water and get wrinkled feet?' he asked politely.

Ignoring his obvious amusement, she tipped up her chin and gave him a long, cold stare, staying exactly where she was. 'I thought I was coming to see your father!'

'No, I *told* you, he's in hospital,' he replied with great patience, as if he were talking to a slow-witted child.

'But he rang last night.' Her eyes hardened. 'Didn't he?'

'Yes. He'd been trying to get me at home. They knew at the plantation that I was somewhere in the hotel so they told him to try there.'

'At three in the morning?' she asked scathingly.

'Good grief, he doesn't concern himself with the fact that other people might be asleep!' he exclaimed drily. 'If he's awake he thinks nothing of waking anyone he pleases. He wanted to know if you'd arrived.'

'How is he?' she asked cautiously.

Pascal gave a short, mirthless laugh. 'Like a cornered bull. Yelling at me on the phone and the nurses at the same time. No change in his physical condition, incidentally. He's not supposed to see anyone and he's not supposed to get excited.'

Mandy's brows pulled together. 'You hate him and yet you visit him?'

'He's my father,' Pascal said simply.

She felt a little better about him for saying that. 'What about what you said last night?' she asked suspiciously. 'About solving the situation—'

'That's why you're here. I sent China to get you,' he said smoothly. 'We need time together—uninterrupted time. I used one of my father's cards to entice you because I thought you wouldn't come if you knew we'd be alone on a deserted beach. I had to get you here, Mandy, to tell you something.'

Suddenly the amusement had vanished. Mandy frowned at the seriousness of his warm blue eyes and she felt her pulses quicken in anticipation. But she couldn't trust him. She'd be a fool to do that.

'I don't like your methods,' she said coolly.

'I don't like my father's,' he countered. 'That's why I've had you brought here and why you must, why you deserve to have an explanation.'

Slowly Mandy walked through the silken water to the beach where he stood, so confident, so certain that he was in the right. Perhaps he was—and maybe she should give him the benefit of the doubt. 'It had better be a good one! You've already got some explaining to do about last night!' she muttered, annoyed that he'd managed to deceive her so easily. He must think her very naïve. Her mouth tightened. 'How do you think it looked, with me wrapped in a sheet and you in my villa in the early hours looking all dishevelled?'

'Damning?' he suggested tentatively.

'I'm darned if I can tell if you're as innocent as you make out or not!' she muttered. 'If you've deliberately ruined my reputation then I want to know why! And if it was a total accident you've got some explaining to do at the hotel on my behalf. I'm not sitting through another breakfast there and having a plate of smoked salmon and scrambled eggs dumped in front of me by a disapproving waitress who thinks I'm flighty!'

'I'm sorry,' he sympathised, sounding remarkably sincere. 'I can assure you that you won't have to go through that experience again.' He looked contrite. 'I admit that I had hoped to soften you with a little alcohol but I had no idea Simon was going to bring you two drinks—or that you'd knock them back so fast. Did I?'

'You could have told him to bring two Voodoo Punches when you chatted with him. You were very buddy-buddy with him.'

'I should hope so. He's the son of my overseer,' said Pascal surprisingly. 'But I've known him since he was a baby. I wouldn't dream of using him like that and ordering him to tell lies for me.'

'All right. I accept your explanation about the drinks,' she said grudgingly. 'But it seems to me that you knew your father was going to ring—and that's why you hung around in my villa all night, waiting for someone to appear and find us together!'

Pascal shrugged. 'I honestly had no idea he'd call.' He looked at her in a puzzled way. 'You do care what people think of you, do you?'

When she nodded miserably his face softened. She thought that he was going to touch her in reassurance, but instead he thrust his hands deep into his shorts pockets.

'I do my best to lead a decent life,' she said quietly.

It seemed that she'd surprised him by that remark. He pushed his hand through his silky blond hair. 'We must try to make sure that you do,' he drawled, his intense cerulean blue eyes fixed on hers. 'Tell me... if you were as embarrassed as you say, why didn't you ask for room service this morning, instead of turning up for breakfast in the restaurant?'

Mandy flipped up her chin. 'And admit I've done something I'm ashamed of?' she said indignantly.

Admiration showed in his eyes and the dimples came out to disarm her. 'You have courage, Mandy,' he said softly. 'I'm impressed. That must have taken some guts.'

'It did. What are you going to do to clear my name?' she asked, feeling mollified.

'Leave everything to me. I'm going to make sure that no one at the hotel treats you with contempt again. I promise.' And he laid a hand on his heart and fixed her with his unblinking gaze.

'Thank you. Make sure you do explain what happened,' she said in relief. 'Now...you said we had to talk. What...what do you have to tell me?' she asked cautiously.

'A rather unpleasant story. I think you'd better come to my house. It's on the plantation next door to Beau Rivage,' he said with a worrying gentleness. 'We'll sit on the deck and have coffee.'

'I can't trust you, Pascal,' she muttered.

'Caught between the devil and the deep blue sea?' He gave a faint smile. 'If you're worried about being alone with me, then forget it. There's a full complement of staff and my aunt lives with me. Shall we go? The Jeep's just up the road.'

'I don't have much choice, do I?' she said wryly.

He touched her shoulder briefly, as someone might when comforting a close friend. 'No, you don't,' he agreed smoothly.

She bit her lip. But Pascal had already cupped her elbow and was guiding her towards the trees. They grew so densely at the back of the beach that the sudden shadow beneath the palms plunged the two of them into a half-darkness.

'Everything looks awfully unkempt,' she commented. 'Does anyone ever use this track?'

'Not often.' Pascal helped her into the Jeep and slammed the door. 'Beau Rivage is reverting to nature,' he explained when he got in beside her. 'It's suffered a few blows in its lifetime—hurricane damage, disease, my father's neglect and his antagonistic attitude towards the association.'

'The association?'

'The Agricultural Association,' he said absently. 'It's the marketing agent for the farmers of St Lucia. The farmers farm, the association buys the crop and sells in bulk. Fall out with the association and you have no market. That's what Father did.'

'You haven't a good word to say about him,' she said in sad reproach.

'I think he's getting his just deserts. You know the old saying—sow the wind, reap the whirlwind. He *is* an unpleasant man, Mandy. I hope you don't discover that personally. You're such a gentle soul and far too nice to get involved with him. It'll be a bumpy ride. Hold on.'

A bumpy ride in what sense? she wondered. But from then on conversation was impossible and the questions on her lips had to wait. She'd only heard one side of the story—Pascal's. His father might have a very different viewpoint and she was looking forward to the time when she eventually met Vincente St Honoré and learnt why she'd been brought to St Lucia. And she was intrigued, she had to admit, to know the truth behind Pascal's hatred of his father.

The Jeep began to sway as it negotiated the ruts and Mandy concentrated on hanging onto the edge of the seat. Pascal's face was set in deep concentration till he sensed that she was watching him and then he turned and grinned ruefully at her.

'It gets worse!' he assured her

'Oh, hurray,' she said wryly, and they both laughed as the Jeep plunged into a huge hole. 'Pro-phet-ic!' she jerked out, the breath leaving her body when they lurched out again.

When she could, she stole surreptitious glances at him, trying to work him out. A warm smile had taken up residence on his sunny face, a new air of energy had stolen into his body. He was happy here, she thought. Totally at home in this amazing place.

And she began to take in her surroundings because she thought that they might give a clue to the man. It was a real tropical wilderness—a jungle so dense and untamed that she felt a little afraid of it. Beside her, bucketing about in his seat, changing gear with a smooth and fluid skill, Pascal was obviously in his element and totally in command.

She looked at him with a new respect. Last night he'd been sophisticated and worldly in his hand-stitched dinner jacket. He inhabited a world of wealth where it was normal to have a crane and a barbecue on your boat.

And yet he was coming alive here, in this amazing jungle, dressed in casual bush clothes and with a wicked-looking cutlass clipped on the dash. This was his environment—exciting, exotic, dramatic, with coconuts lying where they'd fallen on the forest floor, tall, spear-like shoots sprouting from them, enormous stands of bamboo, the canes as thick as Pascal's strong thighs and roaring eighty feet into the sky, and thick lianas dangling Tarzan-style from immense trees.

'Mahogany!' shouted Pascal over the surge of the engine as they struggled up a steep and slippery hill. 'Breadfruit.'

He waved at a tree with enormous green footballs hanging on it and Mandy grinned and nodded. Then she cried out in delight when they crested the hill and drove towards a carpet of flame-coloured flowers that set the ground on fire. She looked up and saw a tree that seemed to touch the sky, ablaze with the gaudy blooms.

'Flame-tree!' He smiled to himself then leaned over to shout, as if he wanted to make sure that she heard every word, 'We use them to mark the end of territory!'

'Nicer than "Keep Off" signs!' she yelled.

They exchanged glances—hers full of joy at the beauty of the jungle, his at first unresponsive to her delight and then softening as if he couldn't help himself. It became a long, intense look. He stopped the Jeep, leaving the engine running, and simply gazed at her. And Mandy felt her breath becoming slower and slower while her heart rate increased rapidly.

'You like it here,' he said slowly.

'I think it's wonderful,' she replied, her eyes shining with emotion.

'Me too,' he said huskily, and he was looking at her intently.

A timeless silence stretched between them. Neither of them seemed able to tear their eyes away from the other and Mandy trembled at the mounting tension and the certainty that he'd reach out any second and take her in his arms. And at that precise moment she wanted him to.

Her eyes grew puzzled. She felt right here. Brought up in cities, moved from one children's home to another, finding a home in the Devon countryside with its hills and valleys and little stone cottages, she was nevertheless quite certain that she too could move around comfortably in this strange, alien environment and even call it home.

A nervous excitement prevaded her whole body. Perhaps it *was* her home. Maybe her ancestors had come over from Scotland as Mr Lacey had suggested and her family had lived in St Lucia—and that was why she felt so *right*!

'Oh, Pascal!' she breathed, overwhelmed by the certainty.

There were fierce lights in his eyes, an emotional hunger that echoed hers. Instead of being afraid of it, she felt more drawn to him than ever. He too knew deep longings. Those pained eyes showed a knowledge of suffering, perhaps as great as hers. The lines around his mouth, his anger, his relationship with his father—all these pointed to a man who had been hurt and was unhappy. A wave of empathy engulfed her and she smiled hesitantly.

'We're close to my plantation, Beau Jardin,' he said quietly. He let out the clutch and with the movement of the Jeep the electrically charged air between them evaporated. 'See the bananas?' he asked prosaically. 'They're on my land.'

A little crestfallen, Mandy dutifully peered ahead, keeping her yearning to be closer to him a total secret.

At first nothing looked different, then she saw a mass of paddle-shaped banana leaves and suddenly they'd driven onto a smooth road and her bones weren't jumping up and down inside her skin any more. But she felt an odd kind of regret that the brief closeness and the strange emotional link between them had vanished.

Since that kind of thinking was unwise, she looked for some bright comment. 'You should sell that track back there to a theme park. A white-knuckle ride over hill and dale,' she said ruefully. 'People pay money for that kind of thing.'

'And lose the wildlife to hundreds of screaming tourists? No, thanks.' He grimaced.

'It's a wonderful wilderness,' she said warmly. 'Anyone who owned it would be the happiest person alive.'

'You covet it,' he said, almost under his breath, and she saw so many emotions chasing over his face that she wasn't sure whether he was glad or disturbed by that fact.

She laughed. 'Anyone would, wouldn't they?'

Pascal's mouth thinned. 'Beau Rivage is the carrot my father dangles as a lure.'

The bitterness in his tone made her slant her eyes at him curiously. 'Do you have brothers or sisters?'

'No.'

'Then it'll be yours one day, surely?'

'I doubt it,' he said curtly. 'Do you see those blue plastic bags around the bananas?'

Mandy gave an inward sigh. It looked as if Pascal was not going to inherit Beau Rivage when his father died. And it was obvious that he wasn't prepared to discuss the matter.

'Yes,' she said, wishing that it were in her power to bring the two men together, and asked as Pascal evidently wanted her to, 'What are they for? They're such an eyesore!'

'Better that than to lose the fruit to tree rats, opossums or birds,' he said. 'They also protect the delicate skin of the young fruit. If we have strong winds or a hurricane, the dry leaves can damage the skins and make them unfit for market.'

'You could use green bags,' she suggested.

He smiled in a friendly way at her. 'Blue reduces the infrared rays of the sun and premature ripening.'

'It's much more complicated than I thought,' she mused.

'Things always are,' he said drily. But he continued to smile as he surveyed the rows and rows of bananas.

'You love this land, don't you? It makes you smile,' she said, touched by the pride in his face.

'I love it,' he said softly.

Expecting to see an old plantation house any minute, she was surprised when Pascal stopped for a moment at the head of a Robinson Crusoe-style beach and pointed

to a white stone house with green tiles perched high on
the cliff, commanding views over the almost land-locked
bay where Pascal's boat lay at anchor.

'My house,' he said simply. 'It belonged to my father's
cousin Louis. A great guy. Louis died about ten years
ago, childless and unmarried, and left Beau Jardin to
me.'

Mandy nodded. 'Adjoining plantations. That must be
a difficult situation, with you and your father at daggers
drawn. Your ancestors were French, presumably?'

'Aristocrats from Versailles. The St Honorés were
given land grants by Louis XVI in 1784 and have farmed
here ever since. The land is our life,' he said softly.

'You mentioned an aunt but not your mother,' she
said, tentatively probing.

'She ran away.' He leaned forward and stared ahead
at the beautiful bay with sightless eyes.

Mandy's attention was completely captured. 'Oh, I'm
sorry,' she said, shocked. 'How old were you?'

'Six. Mother was very much under Father's thumb.
My main recollection of her is that she was a cowed and
nervous woman who never left the house.' The strong
jaw tightened and his mouth took on a hard line from
some awful memory.

His mother had left him. He must have found that
terribly hard to accept. Mandy put her hand on his where
it clenched the steering wheel so tightly that it seemed
as if he meant to crush it, and she felt the steely, straining
sinews of his bare brown arm beneath hers.

'I'm sorry she ran away.' She was careful not to say,
How could a mother leave her child? because that would
have been hurtful. It had happened. Rubbing it in
wouldn't help. 'Were you upset, or angry?'

'Confused. And, yes, I was upset. Not as much as you
might think, though. We were never close so I suppose
it was my pride and my sense of self-worth that suffered.
And I had no wish to go with her. I would have been

miserable living anywhere else,' he said quietly. 'This part of the world means everything to me. It draws me like a magnet. When I'm away I want to come home.'

'I suppose she knew that,' suggested Mandy diplomatically.

He gave a faint smile. 'I suppose she did. She knew how happy I was here. There aren't many places where you can wear nothing but shorts and old trainers all day long, right through the year.'

She nodded, remembering Simon's remark that Pascal wore very little. It certainly gave *her* a great sense of freedom—the thought of just reaching for a T-shirt and shorts each day. 'If she was the nervous type, it must have been hard for her to leave,' she mused. 'It's surprising she had the courage—'

'No.' Pascal was hardly breathing. Mandy watched sympathetically, seeing that his eyes glowed like burning sapphires in his harrowed face. Instinctively she tightened her hand, surrounding the cold, tensed fingers with warmth. 'She was driven out by sheer desperation.'

'Please don't go on—' she began, unwilling to hear of his parents' quarrels.

'You need to know,' he said tightly.

'Why? It can't have any bearing on my purpose here,' she argued uncomfortably.

'It has,' he insisted, and turned to face her, taking her hands in his with an urgent air. 'You need to know about my father,' he said harshly. 'The kind of man he is. That he's a bully and...' He scowled, a deep V appearing between his angry brows. 'I heard my mother screaming—'

'Please! Don't!' she cried, trying to pull away.

'*Listen!*' He jerked her back, his strong brown fingers wrapping around the slender satin of her pearly wrists. 'It's important to me. I want you to know.'

'All right,' she said reluctantly. 'If it'll help.'

'I burst into their room.' Pascal's intense stare held her transfixed. 'He must have hit her because she was on the floor, cringing away from him.' His eyes blazed. 'My father ordered me to my room. When I was eventually allowed to come out my mother had gone.'

'Oh, Pascal!' she cried brokenly, her face filled with compassion. 'How awful! Your poor mother! No wonder she ran away. It must have been dreadful when you realised what had happened. Dreadful. You haven't known what it is to have proper parents at all, have you?' she said sadly, knowing how he must feel.

'I spent most of my time with Louis and with Father's sister, my aunt Susannah. I was happy enough. They were very loving and more than compensated for my parents,' he said quietly. 'I've told you this because it gives you some insight into my father's character. You can see why I don't want you anywhere near him. And that I have good reason to hate him.'

'Yes, but—'

'No buts!' he said sharply. 'You mustn't have anything to do with him—'

'But I *must*! she insisted helplessly.

'No. He's dangerous. You are very innocent and very appealing.'

His eloquent eyes seemed to smoulder and she felt a warmth stealing through her body as his hands eased their grip and, almost unaware that he was doing so, he began to caress her arms, moving his fingers in a compelling rhythm.

'Pascal!' she husked, and found that her throat had closed up. His mouth had softened. It seemed that he dearly wanted to kiss her and she leaned forward almost imperceptibly, her lips parting.

'Hell!' he muttered, frowning. 'You're a little witch! For the last time, Mandy, will you go home today, tomorrow, or not?'

AN IMPORTANT MESSAGE FROM THE EDITORS OF HARLEQUIN®

Dear Reader,

Because you've chosen to read one of our fine romance novels, we'd like to say "thank you"! And, as a **special** way to thank you, we've selected <u>four more</u> of the <u>books</u> you love so well, **and** a beautiful Cherub Magnet to send you absolutely *FREE!*

Please enjoy them with our compliments...

Candy Lee

Editor, Presents

P.S. And because <u>we value</u> our customers, we've attached something extra inside ...

EDITOR'S
FREE
GIFT
SEAL
THANK YOU

PEEL OFF SEAL AND PLACE INSIDE

HOW TO VALIDATE
YOUR
EDITOR'S FREE GIFT
"THANK YOU"

1. Peel off gift seal from front cover. Place it in space provided at right. This automatically entitles you to receive four free books and a lovely Cherub Magnet.

2. Send back this card and you'll get brand-new Harlequin Presents® novels. These books have a cover price of $3.50 each, but they are yours to keep absolutely free.

3. There's no catch. You're under no obligation to buy anything. We charge nothing — ZERO — for your first shipment. And you don't have to make any minimum number of purchases — not even one!

4. The fact is thousands of readers enjoy receiving books by mail from the Harlequin Reader Service® . They like the convenience of home delivery...they like getting the best new novels BEFORE they're available in stores...and they love our discount prices!

5. We hope that after receiving your free books you'll want to remain a subscriber. But the choice is yours — to continue or cancel, anytime at all! So why not take us up on our invitation, with no risk of any kind. You'll be glad you did!

6. Don't forget to detach your FREE BOOKMARK. And remember...just for validating your Editor's Free Gift Offer, we'll send you FIVE MORE gifts, *ABSOLUTELY FREE!*

This charming refrigerator magnet looks like a little cherub, and it's a perfect size for holding notes and recipes. Best of all it's yours ABSOLUTELY FREE when you accept our NO-RISK offer!

THE EDITOR'S "THANK YOU"
FREE GIFTS INCLUDE:

▶ Four BRAND-NEW romance novels
▶ A beautiful Cherub Magnet

PLACE
FREE GIFT
SEAL
HERE

YES! I have placed my Editor's "thank you" seal
in the space provided above. Please send me 4 free
books and a lovely Cherub Magnet. I understand I am
under no obligation to purchase any books, as explained
on the back and on the opposite page.

106 CIH CCLA (U-H-P-09/97)

NAME

ADDRESS   APT.

CITY   STATE   ZIP

Thank you!

DETACH AND MAIL CARD TODAY!

THE HARLEQUIN READER SERVICE®: HERE'S HOW IT WORKS

Accepting free books places you under no obligation to buy anything. You may keep the books and gift and return the shipping statement marked "cancel". If you do not cancel, about a month later we will send you 6 additional novels, and bill you just $2.90 each plus 25¢ delivery per book and applicable sales tax, if any*. That's the complete price, and—compared to cover prices of $3.50 each—quite a bargain! You may cancel at any time, but if you choose to continue, every month we'll send you 6 more books, which you may either purchase at the discount price…or return to us and cancel your subscription.

*Terms and prices subject to change without notice. Sales tax applicable in N.Y.

'How can I?' she mumbled in distress, confused by her feelings. 'You know what I want. Whether I like it or not, I have to—'

'As you wish,' he interrupted coldly.

It was such a shame. Her heart had been touched by his story and she wanted to share some of her own loneliness with him because he, too, seemed to be alone in the world. He wasn't wearing a wedding ring, she noticed, although a man as charismatic as Pascal must have a partner, she realised, if not several.

But all her desires to ease the misery of his childhood were being thwarted by his stubborn demand that she should go home. How could she when his father held the key to her past? She didn't want to clash head-on with Pascal, not now. But it seemed as if she was destined to do so.

'Pascal,' she said, upset, 'you must understand. I have to do this—'

Pascal snatched his hands away so angrily that she shut her mouth and didn't press the point. Already he'd set the gears screaming as he reversed for a short distance and then drove at a furious pace up the road that led to the house on the cliff.

Mandy felt a great disappointment—and a fear that sat in her stomach like a heavy lump. She wasn't looking forward to meeting his father in the near future. If her mission wasn't so important, she'd turn tail and run.

Sadly she clambered out of the Jeep when it came to a halt in front of the handsome, green-jalousied house. The air was scented with jasmine and jewel-like hummingbirds were hovering over the hibiscus bushes on the lawn.

'I understand your feelings,' she said gently. 'You must understand mine.' He didn't answer and her heart ached for him because his face was dark with bitterness as he stood beside her on the edge of the black cliff. 'You're still annoyed with me,' she said unhappily. 'But see it from my point of view—'

'I thought better of you, Mandy,' he said in a low voice. 'I thought that you had understood how rash you'd be to insist on meeting my father.'

'He can't hurt me—'

'Oh, he could. He's a bitter man intent only on his own selfish pleasures and without a care for the welfare or the feelings of others.'

'I have to see him,' she said quietly. 'It wasn't easy for me, coming all this way, Pascal. I've never travelled abroad before. It was all quite unnerving, managing on my own. Doesn't that tell you how important this is to me? I wish you'd tell me the real reason you want me to leave. Is it because your father will get some kind of reward if I turn up and you want to deprive him of that?'

He gave her a brief, cynical glance. 'Sure he'll get a reward if you turn up. That's obvious, isn't it? And yes, I want to deprive him of it. Of you.'

She felt disappointed that Pascal was putting all his energies into revenge. Somehow it didn't seem the kind of thing he'd do, but he'd admitted as much. Perhaps if they talked a little more she might persuade him to let things take their course. If he understood something of her background, he might feel a little different.

She lifted her head to the sea breeze, determined to work things out amicably, as he'd suggested earlier. 'Thank you for being so frank,' she said. His mouth twisted. 'I don't want to be your enemy, Pascal,' she said hesitantly.

'Nor I yours.' He turned his magnetic gaze on her and she felt the surrender of some part of herself to the hint of longing in his steady look. 'I would like to know you, really know you. I'd like to show you my island. To spend the next few days with you—'

'We can do that, Pascal.' She smiled dreamily, thinking how much she'd like that. 'I'd like that. The view is out of this world,' she said softly, hoping to reach his heart.

'Oh, yes,' he said softly.

She sighed, hearing again the deep love he had for the place. It was such a pity that he and his father were enemies. They ought to be sharing the beauty of it all. Turning around, she took in the panorama of the two Piton peaks beyond and the broad sweep of rainforest-covered mountains filling half the sky. 'Nothing but jungle and mountains on one side and the sea on the other,' she said in awe.

'It's very remote,' he agreed, and then gave her a thoughtful glance which chilled her because his eyes seemed remote too. 'My banana plantation is surrounded by a vast belt of jungle. And that is backed by miles of rainforest and precipitous mountains. There's only one good road out—and that's blocked by a landslide at the moment. We had a lot of rain last month.'

Mandy detected the note of warning in his tone and tried not to let her nervousness show. She didn't need to be afraid. And yet, undeniably, she was.

'There must be other ways out,' she said, reassuring herself. 'You have to get the bananas to market somehow, don't you?'

'Yes. By sea. That's how they used to transport the sugar cane in the old days. The bananas are cut every Tuesday and Wednesday, boxed and brought down by trucks to the beach. So this house is only accessible by water at the moment. Otherwise it's cut off from the world.' His voice had grown quiet, but there was a slight edge to it, as if he wanted to drive a point home.

'Do your staff *live* here, then?' she asked. She was silly to feel faintly threatened. He'd said that there were people here. His aunt, too.

'Oh, yes.' He glanced down at her but it was a strange, contemplative look, and she felt a quiver of uncertainty run through her. 'And they're stuck here till the boat comes. They know how dangerous it would be to attempt to walk out, you see.' He let that sink in and then, 'Let's have some coffee, shall we?' he suggested casually.

One or two St Lucians were bustling about on the wide terrace, otherwise Mandy might have held back, because Pascal's tone had been so unnerving. And nagging in her brain was the knowledge that she couldn't leave unless he wanted her to. It seemed that she'd be there till one of them capitulated. It seemed even more important that she confided some of her life history to him and gained his sympathy.

Unless, of course, he was deceiving her again and his protestations of danger were an elaborate pretence.

Following a step or two behind him, she said, 'Aren't you being a little over-dramatic about the dangers here? There aren't any tigers here, after all,' she joked, deliberately making herself mock her own fears.

'No. But this isn't some English bluebell wood either, and there are other dangers,' he said drily over his shoulder.

As he reached the veranda she caught up with him and held his arm, looking up at him with anxious eyes. 'What do you mean?'

He shrugged. 'There's always a risk of being bitten by the fer-de-lance snake. It's deadly—though admittedly shy and rarely seen. I've never come across any, but they're out there nevertheless. And a young boy was killed last month by one,' he said. 'Perhaps you should see what else lies in the rainforest for unwary wanderers. Jean-Paul! *Le serpent*!'

Mandy's eyes rounded. A young man came from around the corner of the house with a huge snake wrapped around his forearm. 'Wow!' she exclaimed. 'What's...that?'

'A boa constrictor. An eight-footer. *Merci*, Jean-Paul.' Pascal took the huge snake carefully, fitting his hand

gently around its throat with his thumb on the head.
The snake wound its body around Pascal's muscular
brown arm while Mandy watched with fascination.
'There are quite a few of these around,' he added.

She saw the coils tightening. 'You're kidding me,' she
said calmly. 'I'm sure they don't live in the West Indies.
It's a pet, isn't it?'

'No. It's wild. Aren't you scared?' he asked, a little
taken aback by her interest.

'Not in the least,' she said airily, her mouth twitching
in uncontrollable delight at his disappointment. If this
was his attempt to scare her, it had fallen flat! 'Snakes
have never bothered me. I think it's lovely.' With a gentle
hand she touched the firm, dry body and felt the muscles
working beneath the skin. 'What a beautiful creature.
It's awfully heavy,' she said, testing the weight of its coils.
'And look, the scales are iridescent,' she cried in wonder.

'Don't put your face near its head,' he said abruptly.
'It'll sense your heat. And don't be fooled by the way
I'm handling this. The boas are very dangerous—'

'Should you be holding it?' she asked, widening her
eyes innocently.

'It's been fed,' he said, frowning as if annoyed by her
lack of squeamishness. 'Jean-Paul gave it a rat this
morning.' Pascal handed the snake back to the young
man and she saw the ribbed pressure marks on his arm
where the flesh had been squeezed. 'I'm showing you
this because I thought you might not believe me if I said
there were boa constrictors in the jungle,' he said stiffly.

'You were right,' she retorted sweetly.

He shrugged and watched Jean-Paul set the snake on
the ground. It headed for the nearest undergrowth and
in a moment it was lost from view. 'There are plenty
more out there,' he said sternly. 'Remember that. You
mustn't go off on your own. Do you understand?'

'I won't have to,' she said with a confidence she didn't feel. 'Because soon you'll be taking me back the way we came, won't you?'

'I'm sure I will,' he said gravely. 'Now come and have coffee and banana chips.'

Mandy followed him onto the veranda and curled up on the soft green cushions of a large rattan chair. 'Why did you keep the snake?' she asked, munching on a chip. 'To scare off unwelcome visitors? To unnerve trembling women and render them vulnerable?'

His mouth compressed but he didn't deny her accusation. 'I wouldn't keep a wild animal in captivity,' he answered flatly, passing her a wafer-thin china cup filled with aromatic coffee.

'So what was the pantomime about the snake supposed to mean? What did you intend to do with it? What if I *had* screamed and fallen in a feminine heap at your feet?'

'Then you would have been conveniently vulnerable and I would have bargained with you,' he said, as if he'd behaved in the most reasonable way possible.

'You'd use a *dumb animal*—?' she spluttered, almost beside herself in anger.

'The snake has been set free unharmed, and well fed. It has served its purpose without suffering any stress.' He eyed her with his piercing blue eyes. 'Captivity must only be used as a last resort.'

A silence fell. This time it was menacing. Pascal's steely gaze held hers as surely as if she'd been clasped in the snake's coils. But suddenly Pascal looked the more dangerous. She wanted to ask whose captivity he was referring to, but she wasn't sure she wanted to know the answer.

Moodily she broke up some chips and threw them for the grackles. He wanted her off the island and he'd do anything to achieve that—even to the extent of threatening her with a snake. Most women would have been terrified. She shivered, alarmed at the lengths he'd go to.

So what would he do now? He was lounging back in his chair like a lord, totally relaxed, utterly confident, and projecting a rather unnerving and sinister menace.

She swallowed. Aware that he watched her every movement, she tried to marshal her thoughts and to look casual as she concentrated on feeding a bird with a deformed bill, making sure it had the most food because she felt sorry for it. Sensing Pascal's amusement, she shot him a defiant look from under her lashes.

'It won't survive without help,' she explained firmly, defying him to laugh at her sentimentality.

'Nor will you.' He studied the squabbling birds cynically and then turned his hard blue eyes on her.

'I don't believe the jungle is crawling with snakes,' she said crossly.

'Let me tell you something,' he said quietly. 'Before the days of the sugar plantations and slavery there weren't any snakes. The fer-de-lance were introduced by the slave-masters to stop the slaves from escaping into the jungle. Unfortunately, an overseer was bitten.'

'Good,' she said brutally, wondering why she was getting a lesson in island history.

'So they brought in the mongoose.' His mouth quirked. 'Which ate the chickens and their eggs. So—'

'They brought in the boa constrictors,' finished Mandy. 'Yes. OK. I believe you. There are snakes out there. Nobody could invent a story like that.'

'It's amazing how a single action can create a complex series of events,' mused Pascal. 'One decision, led by greed, can lead to desperate measures. But don't underestimate the dangers of the present situation, Mandy,' he added.

'Dangerous for the boas, for you or for me?' she asked, her expression resentful.

He smiled faintly. 'Mainly you. You're in unknown territory, aren't you? The snakes and I know how to take care of ourselves out here. There are boas in the rainforest which are four times the size of the one you've seen. And they'll kill you if they're hungry. Nature—raw in tooth and claw.'

'I've got the message,' she said, more perkily than she felt. 'Don't go off for a walk without taking a few rats with you.' She gave him a pointed look and he laughed softly, correctly interpreting her meaning. He was a rat and ought to be fed to the snakes! 'However, since I'm being driven back to the beach after coffee so that the Rastafarian—China, isn't it?—can take me in his boat to the hotel, I don't need to concern myself with the dangers of jungle hiking, do I?' she asked in direct challenge.

Pascal looked down at his coffee thoughtfully and swirled it around the delicate cup while she held her breath. 'That depends,' he admitted, lifting his cynical gaze to meet her startled eyes.

'You're not seriously thinking of keeping me here!' she cried in a shaky voice. 'You said you knew how to solve this situation—'

'True.' He flicked a banana chip to the crossbilled grackle. Much to Mandy's distress, the other birds descended on it, their long, sharp beaks pecking at the crossbill till it flew away. 'That bird would survive better in captivity and so would you.' His smile of regret chilled her to the bone. 'I'm sorry it's come to this, Mandy, but you need protection,' he said softly. 'And the only option I have left is to shut you away, free from all harm.'

CHAPTER SIX

'PASCAL! No!' Mandy leapt to her feet in alarm, knocking over the chair. 'You can't do that! Why, your aunt would throw a fit—'

'Oh, didn't I tell you?' His thick eyebrows lifted in exaggerated surprise. 'She's not here today. Shopping, I believe, in Castries. She may stay on. We have a house there she uses.'

The cup dropped from her lifeless fingers. There was an air of cool determination in Pascal's manner and she knew that he had every intention of holding her on the plantation till she did whatever he wanted.

Horrified at his plan, she whirled around and fled into the house, looking for someone to protect her, flinging open doors, catching glimpses of male occupation, of comfort and luxury. Muted silks, gleaming antique furniture, huge oil paintings, silver gleaming in shuttered rooms, cool breezes from paddle fans, and everywhere the scent of the exotic flower displays.

And then, near the back of the house, she heard voices, and ran towards them till she found herself in a large, airy kitchen.

'Oh, thank heavens! Help me!' she cried to the startled women chopping vegetables at stainless-steel worktops. 'Help me get away!' she sobbed. She searched for some French. '*Aidez-moi! Au secours—appelez la police!* I'm in trouble. I'm being...' Her voice trailed off. Their faces were cold, contemptuous, disgusted. 'Why?' she rasped. 'Why are you looking at me like that?'

There wasn't any point in translating her words. They knew what she was saying and they didn't care. She stood there, shaking. What had he told them? What lies had he twisted into some kind of awful story that made them so hostile? She cringed under the united loathing. To her horror and dismay, each of the women deliberately turned her back and continued chopping.

With a strangled cry Mandy ran for the door to find a telephone, but she fell into Pascal's arms instead and he wrapped them around her like the coils of an iron snake.

'Let me go!' she yelled hysterically, hitting at him in blind rage. 'What you're suggesting is ridiculous! Let me go; let me go!'

Ignoring her pleas, he picked her up roughly as if she were a bundle of old clothes. Struggling and screaming, appalled that the staff were ignoring her cries, she suffered his crushing grip while he grimly climbed a grand staircase.

'Save your breath,' he said levelly over her yells. 'Or I'll stop it for you!'

'How?' she rasped.

He stopped. Stared at her, his eyes glowing. She gasped, sensing the flare of his sexual desire as she gazed up at him with limpid eyes, her lips parted from her sharply indrawn breath. Clutched to his chest, she became intensely aware of him. The way his heart beat beneath her hand—as erratically as hers. The way time seemed to be standing still and yet, inside her body, simmered something quite unstoppable.

'Hell.' He bent his head in a sudden movement. Kissed her fiercely. Released her suddenly. And, wondering what he intended, she began to tremble visibly in his arms. 'Behave, please,' he said gruffly, kicking open a door.

A bedroom. A bed. Her eyes darted around the darkened room. What she could see was very masculine and very grand. Pascal's bedroom, without a doubt. 'No!' she whispered, seeing that Pascal was locking the door and excluding the little light that had entered from the landing. And she could say no more.

'I'll just run through one or two points of interest,' Pascal murmured. He slid her to the ground and lit tall candles in an ornate candelabra on the wide window-sill, illuminating scarlet shot silk hangings on the four-poster and pale sand walls.

Mandy gulped and fought her terror. 'Let me go!' she snapped, contradicting her apparently brave stand against him by backing away warily as he advanced to the bed.

'There are hurricane shutters on the windows here and in the bathroom,' he said briskly. 'There's no way out, Mandy. So you'll have to—'

'No! I'll yell and your staff will relent—'

'They know what I'm doing and they are fully behind me,' he replied with shocking calmness.

Astounded, she checked her cry of horror, reached for the alabaster lamp by the bedside, ripped the plug from the socket and brandished the lamp in warning. 'Come near me and I'll brain you!' she seethed.

'I can get what I want,' he said, 'merely by keeping you here. I'm going to do some work. I'll call in at din-nertime to see if you're more tractable.'

'I won't be tractable!' she stormed. 'You can't keep me here! And—and dinnertime's *hours* away!'

'You wouldn't listen to reason. I had no choice. This is for—'

'My own good?' she raged. 'It's not! It's not, Pascal! You know I'm desperate to see your father! It's a dream I'm not going to give up... Oh! Where are you *going*?'

He'd detached himself from the bedpost, shrugged in-differently and had begun to walk to the door. 'Your release is in your own hands.'

'In my own hands... Like this?' Edging towards hys-teria, Mandy threw the lamp at the full-length mirror

and shattered it. He paused briefly, then calmly un-
locked the door and went out.

Furious, she grabbed a nearby chair as well and hurled
it at the door with all her might. It thudded to the wooden
floor, leaving marks on the paintwork. Pascal must have
heard the crash, but he didn't appear to investigate and
a moment later she heard him going down the stairs.

'Oh, *hell*!' she fumed. 'Oh, hell, oh, hell, oh, *hell*!'

There wasn't much else to throw. The room was, despite its grandeur, surprisingly bare. Just the bed, the
chair and a heavy wardrobe that would have needed, she
decided ruefully, the massed bands of the Coldstream
Guards to shift it.

'Bathroom.'

She ran in. Nothing. Only the fixtures themselves and
a couple of large white bathtowels, soap and sachets of
bath oil. Not even a satisfyingly large jar of salts to hurl.
And she might have to entertain herself in the semi-dark
for the next eight hours or so!

'Brute!' she yelled. Feeling that she wanted to let off
steam, she stormed back into the bedroom, hauled the
pillows off the bed and ripped the covers, scattering
feathers everywhere.

Afterwards she surveyed the mess guiltily. It wasn't
like her to lose control like that and spoil perfectly decent
things. 'Oh, drat it!' she moaned, rather shaken by her
uncharacteristic behaviour. Since she'd met Pascal, far
too much had happened inside her body and her mind
for her liking. Too many emotions had erupted. And
Pascal seemed hell-bent on driving her to distraction.
Why?

Now she knew that he wasn't doing this for her own
good. He stood to lose something if she met his father.
Something very important. But she had no idea what it
might be.

In an attempt to come to terms with the prospect of
a few hours of boredom, she paced up and down rest-

lessly, wondering how she could amuse herself. Prowling around, she opened the wardrobe and found some old fashion magazines. They weren't her usual sort of reading but they kept her occupied.

At one o'clock there was the sound of a key in the lock and the handle turned. Mandy warily reached for the lamp but a young woman came in with a tray, put it on the floor and walked out before Mandy could gather her wits. The woman had seen the mess, the feathers in heaps everywhere... and yet she hadn't even raised an eyebrow! A chill ran through her. It was almost as if this had happened before.

The meal looked enticing. She ate the rich chicken and the exotically arranged fresh fruit and spent the next four hours feeling terminally bored, re-reading the magazines and wishing that she had something to do—even crossing swords with Pascal.

At six there was a knock on the door—a knock!—and Pascal appeared. He wore the devastatingly flattering dinner jacket and Mandy had to work hard not to find him attractive. 'Are you all right?' he enquired, sounding almost concerned.

'I'm bored,' she said flatly, refusing to be swayed by the beautiful curve of his chiselled mouth or the drowsy regard of his deep blue eyes.

'Dinner is in one hour,' he announced. He scanned the room, briefly noting the scattered feathers as if her tantrum didn't surprise or interest him in the least. 'Amuse yourself by changing,' he suggested laconically.

She stared at her case which he'd pushed forward with his gleaming black shoe. 'You... you got that from the hotel?' she gasped.

'I had it brought over.' He gave her a faint smile and she found herself watching for the dimples, but none appeared.

'Oh, no!' she groaned. 'They'll think I'm...' Mandy couldn't bring herself to say it.

So Pascal said it for her. 'Shacking up with me,' he said crudely. 'Yes, I did think they might.'

'You said you'd make sure my reputation was cleared!' she said furiously.

'You will keep misinterpreting what I say,' he admonished. 'When you complained about being given the cold shoulder at breakfast-time in the hotel, I said I'd make sure you wouldn't have to go through that experience again. And you won't. I'll see to that—by keeping you here till you leave for England.'

'I see,' she said grimly, and blushed to think of the gossip back at the hotel, which, if Pascal had his way, she'd never hear and never have to face. He'd kept his word—but not as she'd wanted.

So where did that leave her? Stuck here. Then forced to leave the country because her time had run out. She felt her lip quiver. 'Why are you doing this to me?' she asked miserably.

'You know why. Get changed,' he said, frowning.

But there was something in his eyes that didn't match his abrupt order. And the more he gazed at her pale face and enormous, soft hazel eyes, the more she knew that he had a reason of his own. She licked her lips nervously and gulped when he drew in a ragged breath that parted his sensual lips as if he had been suddenly stricken with hunger. Her breathing became shallow and his gaze was drawn to the deep pulse in her throat and then, like a magnet, to her breasts. Which she protected with her crossed arms.

'Change? And have you walk in on me while I'm in the shower? No way,' she said shakily, appalled at the languor creeping through her body at the thought of his touch.

Pascal finished his approving contemplation of her breasts and said with an infinitely appealing huskiness, 'You're perfectly safe. There's only an hour before dinner. That isn't anywhere *near* long enough for me. I hope that calms your fears. Be ready by seven. We're eating outside and Anne-Marie's worked all afternoon to produce something special.'

When he'd gone she stared at the panelled mahogany door in confusion, her heart beating so fast that she pressed her hand over it as if to hold it still. She'd been scared. That was what he'd intended. What she'd interpreted as her own arousal was only a surge of fear. She ought to be relieved that he wasn't going to make a pass. Yet she knew that her overwhelming feeling was one of rejection. Her mouth tipped up wryly. She had a strong, physical attraction to Pascal; that she couldn't deny. She wanted him to find her irresistible—and yet to resist her! Stupid!

In an hour they'd be eating dinner. She had to cling to the hope that she'd be able to persuade him to let her go—although it was clear she'd have to spend a night here. No boat would take her out now. And if she couldn't persuade him? It didn't bear thinking about.

So she tried to think positively. He had a kind heart, she was sure of that. She'd try to reach it. Over dinner she'd tell him her story, leaving nothing out. And he'd understand.

At seven she waited impatiently for Pascal, stalking up and down the room like a caged jungle cat. Her hands checked the brutally prim bun at the nape of her neck with satisfaction, knowing that the style was neither sweetly innocent nor accidentally seductive on this occasion; her thick mane of hair gleamed as if it were polished wood, shaping to her skull like a smooth cap.

There was nothing overtly sensual about her pale aqua cotton dress either. It flowed politely over her body, revealing nothing of its contours, and the only make-up she wore was soft pink lipstick.

But vanity had made her ditch the flat pumps to try on a pair of frivolous high heels and the minute she teetered uncertainly on them she knew that they made a difference to her little-Miss-Prim appearance. Walking could only be accomplished smoothly by a hip-swinging stride that swished the material hungrily around her breasts, her hips and her alarmingly exposed legs.

'You look absolutely stunning,' Pascal said softly when he walked in at that moment.

Mandy frowned at herself in the mirror. She could keep still all evening or walk like a robot... 'I wasn't supposed to.'

Pascal laughed. 'You'd find it difficult to be ugly,' he murmured with deep appreciation. 'Yes. You're very beautiful tonight. Far too beautiful for a man's peace of mind. Coming?'

Lowering her lashes hastily, she followed, resisting the voice of wisdom that told her to put the pumps back on again. She had to hide her expression because she felt insanely pleased by the compliment and wanted to grin smugly in self-satisfaction.

Mandy groaned inwardly. Pascal made her feel more female, more sexually aware of herself and more beautiful than she had with any other man... She bit her lip. Even Dave. Her teeth clenched and she tried to call Dave's beloved face back to mind. Yet Pascal's intense charisma overwhelmed her memories. He was here, and now, right beside her, alive and vibrant with life. And she was betraying the man she'd loved even by feeling flattered that Pascal liked the way she looked.

He held out his hand and before she knew it she'd taken it and he was leading her down the stairs. The beautiful hall, the highly polished antiques, the glorious flower displays and old oil paintings gave her a sense of elegance and she became caught up in the dream, imagining herself in the role of a fashionable lady.

It was nice to dream. Nice to imagine.

When they came through the jalousied doors to the terrace, Mandy gave an involuntary gasp of pleasure and clasped her hands in delight. 'Flares! Lighting the garden! What a lovely idea!'

He smiled warmly, releasing his deep dimples. 'Thank you. We're eating by the water—my favourite place.'

'Very romantic,' she said drily.

He shrugged. 'We could eat in your room if you prefer.'

'Bit feathery,' she countered.

He grinned. 'The water it is, then.'

Mandy nodded and let him tuck her hand over his arm. It didn't matter that she was enjoying the walk between the blazing torches that were stuck into the soil on either side of the path, or that the perfumes of the garden were intoxicating her senses. She would adore the black warmth of the night and the crystal-sharp stars without compromising her position.

If Pascal thought he'd coax her into leaving—or into his bed—by soft lights and the music of a million tree frogs, he was mistaken. She'd admire his garden, eat his meal and remain obdurate. She would win him over to her way of thinking. She knew she would. And she must.

'Roston has laid a table below the garden terraces,' explained Pascal, leading her to the head of a zigzagging path. 'It's not far—you won't spoil your shoes. It's a fairly civilised walk.'

'I don't mind. I got them in a sale. And this is utterly dreamy!' admitted Mandy, catching sight of the ink-black sea. A little way below she could see a glow and when they came nearer saw that the light came from two large candelabra on a table, set on a deck that had been built out over the water. It was so impossibly romantic that she stiffened a little, to stop herself from being swamped by the magic of the night.

'I want you to like my garden.' Pascal plucked a peach-coloured hibiscus and tucked it solemnly in her hair.

'I do,' she said a little breathily, because he smelt so good and he looked achingly handsome. His hair was like a golden halo in the flickering torchlight and his tanned skin a dark contrast to his white shirt and dinner jacket. He was so close. So touchable. 'It won't make any difference,' she told him, her face serious. 'I'm not changing my mind. I know why you're doing this. You think you can win me over. You can't.'

For a long second or two his smile lingered on her, his blue eyes glittering brightly. 'We'll see, shall we?' And then he was carefully helping her down the hewn-rock steps to the wooden deck swathed in flowering vines.

With the gentle curl and hiss of the ocean sucking at the sand in the background, she settled in the lavishly carved chair that he held out for her. Silently he filled her crystal glass with wine. The candlelight made the crystal sparkle; the silver gleamed. Delicate pink flowers, which Herbert had called 'the chain of love', lay strewn artfully across the crisp white linen. She took a cautious sip of the wine and wondered what Pascal's next step would be, steeling herself to kill the blissful atmosphere if necessary and refuse any suggestion he made.

'We won't talk business during dinner,' he said firmly, reading her thoughts. 'It's a deplorable habit and ruins the taste buds. I do have French blood, remember. I thought we'd enjoy the meal, talk about non-controversial things, and then come down to brass tacks afterwards. How's that?'

'Fine by me,' she said casually. 'You could have saved yourself the bother, though. I'm not objecting to the full treatment, because I'm starving, but you could have passed me bread and water through the keyhole and had the same result with less effort.'

He laughed. 'Really?' he said, as if he didn't believe that she'd be able to resist his charm.

'I'm not going to be bullied or coaxed, Pascal, and that's final.'

His blue eyes gleamed with amusement. 'I'm not going to bully or coax you.'

She gazed at him warily. 'Then what—?'

'After dinner,' he said firmly. 'We'll discuss it after dinner.'

Mandy snapped her brows together in irritation, then became aware of someone at her side. The young woman who'd brought her lunch was sliding a plate of seafood in front of her. 'Thank you,' Mandy said, giving the woman a warm smile of appreciation. But all she got in return was a stony look. The smiles were reserved for Pascal, who was evidently adored. 'What have you told them about me?' she demanded crossly.

'Nothing.' Pascal jabbed a piece of lobster with his fork and scooped up some of the tangy sauce. 'I didn't have to.'

'But—'

'Tell me about yourself. Describe your life in England.'

She growled under her breath and toyed with her glass. She could either remain silent and glum through the whole meal or make conversation. It was obvious that Pascal would only talk about her situation when it was over.

'I live in a small cottage in a village. You already know what I do,' she said flatly.

'So tell me about it. Explain why you chose your line of work.'

Bristling at his disapproving tone, she decided to do just that. 'Lack of choice. I don't have any desirable academic qualifications and there's high unemployment in Devon. I was lucky to get the job. It means odd hours, of course, but you get used to that. I like meeting people and chatting to the lonely ones. There's an old lady on my round—'

'A *lady*? On your what?' He frowned at her.

'My round,' she said in surprise. She broke off a piece of bread and chewed it. 'Anyway, she doesn't get many letters. Only bills. So when I have advertising bumf to deliver she's delighted—'

'Wait a minute!' he said sharply, his butter knife poised in mid-air. 'What do you mean, letters?'

She looked as puzzled as he. 'You said you knew about my job. You were pretty scathing about it!' she reminded him huffily. 'Personally, I see nothing wrong in being a postmistress.'

He seemed lost for words. 'A postmistress! You deliver mail? I thought you did something else. I . . . seem to have jumped to the wrong conclusion about you,' he said after a while. 'What did you do before that?'

She made a face. 'I worked as a booking clerk in Plymouth. But I didn't like being in a city.'

Pascal knitted his brows. 'You did answer my father's advert, didn't you?'

'Yes! Otherwise why would I be here? I don't understand, Pascal—'

'Neither do I.' He seemed to be lost in thought.

'In such a rural area as where I work, my job is more than a delivery service,' she said earnestly. 'It links people together. I bring news from one farm to another. I finish early and sometimes I get a bit of shopping in for someone who's housebound or ill. There are lonely people out there, you see. I like chatting to them and we chew over some of their problems. They seem ready to confide in me and I'm happy to provide a sympathetic ear.'

His blue eyes narrowed. 'Such a lot of effort! A huge expenditure on your part in time and energy and emotion. You get something in return, I imagine?'

'Oh, yes!' She smiled gently. 'An enormous amount. Their friendship. We exchange Christmas cards. Sometimes I bring them some flowers from my garden; sometimes they give me half a dozen eggs or a few carrots. Or some cabbage plants.'

'Amazing!' he said faintly.

'No, that's how it is in isolated places. We trade with what we have. I can give them my time, my attention and my interest; they... well, it's like... like having a big family,' she said with a wistful expression. 'But...' She pressed her lips together and concentrated fiercely on unnecessarily sorting prawns from shrimps.

'But?' he prompted huskily.

And when she looked up her sad expression softened into smiles because he seemed genuinely interested and sympathetic. Now she felt that there was hope. He'd begin to understand if she could only explain what it meant to her to trace her family. But it was hard to put into words and she took a while to get her thoughts together. Pascal waited patiently as if he knew that.

Pushing her plate away, she sighed deeply. 'It goes back to the time when I worked for the ferry company,' she said, her voice almost inaudible. 'I was handling the bookings to France. I was stuck indoors all the time. Dave...' She reached out for her glass, fortified herself with wine and then stared vacantly into space. Dave had been so kind. Thoughtful. How could she ever find a man who'd be so good to her?

'Dave?' prompted Pascal.

'Oh. Yes. My husband. He was alive then,' she said with a sigh. 'He knew I felt trapped being indoors so much. We went out every weekend, driving up and down the lanes together, enjoying the countryside and having picnics—even when it was raining. And after he d-died and I lost my job at the booking office because I'd had so much time off I got my present job and had to drive virtually the same routes—'

'And you were continually reminded of the times you'd made those weekend drives together. And the memories were painful to you,' broke in Pascal softly.

'Yes! That's absolutely it!' Surprised that he'd made the connection, she lifted her forlorn face to his, her unshed tears blurring her vision a little. But when she saw that he looked deeply compassionate her mouth trembled in misery. 'I love my job but I find it hard to bear the journeys along the lanes,' she mumbled. 'Every twist and turn holds countless memories. We got to know the lanes so well.'

'A dilemma. How difficult for you. And bitter-sweet.'

Something was pulling her mentally towards him. His compassion, his understanding . . . an indefinable bond of some kind. She didn't know what it was, only that she wanted to confide in him . . . and yet how could he know what it was like to lose someone and to think of him every day, every night?

'I've never spoken about this before,' she blurted out suddenly. 'I don't talk about Dave because it hurts. We were so happy, you see.'

'I'm sure you were. Talk about him now,' he said quietly. 'I want to know and I think you want to talk. It would be a good idea, Mandy.'

'Perhaps.' She stared at the prawns. She'd lined them up to make the letter D. No—the letter P. Startled, she looked up at Pascal from under her lashes. His expression was encouraging. So she assuaged her guilt by eating the tail of the P and decided to open up her heart, as she'd planned earlier.

'Tell me how you met,' he encouraged.

'We'd been in the same children's home together. We'd played together and become friends, hugged one another when we were upset . . . and slowly we'd fallen in love. We married on my eighteenth birthday. He was all the family I ever had, Pascal.' Surely he'd recognise her need? She stared wretchedly at the table, the crystal and silver fusing together in a blur.

Pascal's hand came to cover hers, its warm strength comforting her. 'How did he die?'

It was such a long time since she'd faced up to it and the memory lurched back, as black and brutal as the day she'd sat in her house and stared blankly at the policewoman and Dave's distraught area manager.

She began to sob and Pascal's hand tightened while his thumb massaged the soft web between her thumb and forefinger. 'OK,' he said gently. 'Take it easy. But tell me. I think you should. In your own time.'

She nodded dumbly and after a moment or two felt that she could go on. 'It was his job,' she mumbled between her subsiding sobs. 'He worked f-for the electricity board, and there was an—an accident—'

Pascal stiffened. He'd gone pale beneath his tan, the deep blue eyes standing out fiercely in his bleak face.

'It was awful...such a shock...' she went on. 'I—I didn't expect it, you see. And...' She bit her lip hard. 'I c-can't cope with thinking of his body, all twisted and spoilt...'

'Poor Mandy,' he said huskily. 'I am sorry.'

'I loved him,' she wailed, and he took hold of both her hands then, staring at her helplessly. 'I love him!'

'I understand. I do understand,' he said, sounding choked.

'How can you?' she muttered hopelessly. 'No one could. No one knows what it's like—'

'I do,' he said rawly. 'Because I went through something similar. When my house burnt down.'

Slowly her face lifted. Through her tears she saw the harsh despair in the lines of his mouth, the emptiness in his eyes. And she knew that he too had suffered a tragedy to equal her own. They had a bond. She felt it as strongly as if they'd been linked by love, and it drew them closer together.

'Someone you loved,' she guessed tentatively.

'My wife,' he said in a muted growl. 'My wife and my baby son. They died when my house burnt down.'

And Vincente had started that fire. The tears streamed down her face. There was nothing adequate that she could say. 'Oh—Pascal,' she cried jerkily, and now it was her turn to grip both his hands in sympathy. And that was all she could do until she could clear the huge lump in her throat. 'That was why you attacked your father!'

'I went a little mad. You see, I'd loved them both, more than my life!' he said, the words emerging in one harsh breath.

'I know,' she moaned. 'I know.'

And she forgave him for his behaviour towards his father. The fire had been an accident and Pascal had been misguided to react like that but it was under-standable—dear heaven, it was understandable. He'd suffered more than she'd realised. And he'd been sent to prison for assault, just when he'd lost the two people he'd loved. It was hardly any wonder that Pascal and his father weren't on speaking terms.

It seemed that as they sat there, sharing sympathy and compassion, some of her pain was easing. Pascal was the first person she'd opened up to. Now she sat op-posite an almost total stranger and felt better for shedding some of the burden she'd carried alone.

'I hadn't realised you'd been married,' she said in-consequentially. 'You don't wear a wedding ring.'

'No.'

His eyes meshed with hers, a plain refusal to discuss the matter in the lift of his chin, the directness of his gaze.

'I'm terribly sorry,' she husked, and he nodded as if he'd felt the depth of her compassion in those few, poor words that she'd spoken with such deep sincerity.

'It's... it's the fact you can't share special things with your partner any longer,' she ventured. 'Things that happen to you. Things you want to say that amused you. Things that annoyed you.'

'The desolation,' he said quietly. 'The waste of it. The sheer brutality of the waste of a life. Two lives.' He looked away but she'd seen the betraying shine of fiercely controlled tears in his eyes, and she felt an outpouring of emotion for him.

Their starters were discreetly removed and replaced with something else. Neither of them looked at their plate. Neither of them picked up their fork. They remained silent and still, exchanging a mutual sympathy that Mandy found strangely strengthening.

And after a long, long while she sighed and said gently, 'I'm sorry you've had such a hard time.'

'I'm sorry I've *given* you a hard time,' he answered huskily. 'I seem to have misjudged your character. I can't pretend that I approve of your decision to come over here, but I think we have found a new base to work from. And I know we'll be able to sort this out together. I just know it.'

Hope filled her because he was obviously touched by her situation and would surely help her. She smiled and wiped her eyes. 'I'd like that,' she said fervently.

'I think we should eat.' He cleared his throat and didn't sound so husky when he spoke again. 'That,' he said with slightly forced cheerfulness, pointing to strips of a white vegetable on her plate, 'is christophine.'

She nodded, doing her best to be interested because she recognised that both of them needed to draw back from the intensity of their emotions.

'That's aubergine . . . fried plantain . . . dasheen.'

Mandy did her best. She managed to eat half of the food before she pushed the plate away. 'I've tried but I can't manage any more,' she said in a small voice. 'I can't go on, Pascal! You have to realise what you're doing to my hopes—they're see-sawing up and down and I can't wait any longer. We have to talk. I can't rest till we do.'

'I agree.' He stood up, stretching out his hand. 'I think my appetite has gone too. Shall we walk along the shore?'

Tense and nervous, she went with him down to the beach. Because of the narrowness of the steps she had to follow behind him and her eyes kept drifting to the broad sweep of his shoulders, the narrow hips, the warm strength of his hand as it clasped hers. Quite irrationally she wanted to reach out and smooth her fingers over his back, to feel the softness of his fair hair, the texture, the scent of his skin.

She was muddled. Battered by worry, doubt, fear, weakened by emotion and longing. Longing for Pascal, for his arms, his kisses. Had she said Pascal to herself? She meant Dave. Of course she meant Dave.

And yet... He turned. Smiled gently at her. 'All right?' he asked softly.

'Mmm.'

'You need someone to hold you.' And now that the path was wider he did just that, one arm around her shoulder, holding her as if she'd fall apart if he didn't.

It was nice. More than that. All her instincts were driving her to fling herself into his arms properly, to let him crush her to him, to beg for his kisses—anything to use up the huge surges of emotion that threatened to erupt from her turbulent heart. Pascal understood how she felt and it gave him an unfair advantage over every other man.

She found him deeply attractive as it was. And now that there was this added dimension to him he was proving to be increasingly irresistible. She stole a look at his absorbed face. The moonlight made his skin gleam like burnished gold, the curve of his hair at the nape of his neck extraordinarily appealing to her disordered senses.

They reached the beach and walked along the sand. She tried hard not to let the magical night sway her— the soft rush of waves on the shore, the gentle peace of the bay, the pleasure of at last being with someone who *understood* that terrible emptiness she'd felt, the deafening silence of a house emptied of its laughter, and the starkness of a life spent alone and without an adored spouse's love.

Pascal's grip tightened and she lifted brimming eyes to him, only to discover that he was preoccupied with his own thoughts. 'I know you were hoping for a great deal when you arrived,' he said slowly, as if chewing something over. 'I understand what you were looking for—and why.'

'Then help me,' she begged tremulously.

Still he hesitated. 'I could. I'm not sure I should. My father's illness has been a blow to your plans, hasn't it?' he mused, his steps slowing to a standstill.

'A terrible blow,' she agreed shakily. 'I'd pinned all my hopes on curing my loneliness by coming here.'

She watched the strong jaw tighten, the deep breath that welled up and lifted his powerful shoulders with the force of some private regret. 'So he would have eased your loneliness. You do need protection,' he said wryly. 'From yourself. What would you like me to do?'

Her breath whispered out in a long sigh of relief. He would help her. She knew it. 'After tonight, after all we've shared, I feel I can trust you,' she said earnestly. 'We've exchanged some intimate information about each other. I know about your unhappiness, you know about mine. I understand why you acted as you did, you know why I had no other option but to come here.'

'And so?'

Mandy struggled to avoid the intensity of his smouldering eyes. But she was unable to look away. And she found herself saying breathily, 'There's only one thing I want you to do. And I want it more than anything.' She licked her lips, aware that he was scrutinising her with unnerving concentration. 'Pascal, I know you'll find this a presumption. I know it's not, perhaps, the most orthodox thing to do, but... I want you to take your father's place.'

Pascal stiffened in shock, and he blinked. 'Say that again?'

'Take his place! Please,' she begged fervently. 'Do it for me! It would mean so much to me!' She tugged at his sleeve, her eyes filling with desperate tears when he continued to stare at her, dumbfounded. Surely, as he had the key to his father's house and access to his father's desk, he could search for information about the mysterious client? Why was he being so reticent?

'You can't refuse me,' she said, her voice shaking with emotion. 'You've been determined that I shouldn't become involved with your father. Now I don't have to—not with you around to take care of everything instead. Please!'

He was totally still. Every breath seemed frozen in his body, with only the beat of his heart leaping against her impassioned cheek where she'd pressed it to his chest in a final plea. And she waited, her body as tense as his.

Absently, it seemed, he stroked her hair. 'Do you mean that?' he asked quietly. 'That I should take my father's place?'

Her whole body shuddered with unrelieved strain. 'Oh, yes, yes, Pascal!' she muttered into his shirt.

He tipped up her face and with his thumb wiped away the rolling tears. 'No promises. No strings,' he warned.

'I know,' she croaked. 'I know you can't make any promises. I know I might be disappointed. But I'd rather try it this way than...' Her voice drifted into silence. She was unable to contemplate failure.

'I hope we don't regret this,' he mused, stroking her face with his forefinger. 'But yes. I can't resist you. I don't want to resist you. I agree.'

Mandy beamed in delirious delight through her tears. 'Pascal!' she cried, crying and laughing at the same time. 'Thank you! Thank you!'

'God!' he muttered, and somehow they were both huddled deep in each other's arms.

Mandy sobbed into his chest, reassured by the tightness of his embrace. They'd both been upset—Pascal had intended some brutal revenge on his father that had included her, but now he'd realised that that had been wrong. And he was going to help her to find her family!

'I'm grateful,' she sobbed, her shoulders heaving.

He stroked her back gently and waited for her tears to subside. When she emerged, sheepishly, from his arms and flung him a rueful, elated look, he smiled at her uplifted face and gently kissed her.

To her surprise she found herself kissing him back as if it was the most natural thing in the world. Her arms went around his neck, her fingers laced at the back of his head. Around them the jungle sounds intensified and the waves rushed more fiercely into the beach.

And his mouth drove deeper into hers as if he wanted to drive out the emotion that had been lying in his heart ever since his wife and baby died.

As she thought of his tragedy a huge shuddering breath flowed through her body and she drew his head forward to ease some of her own pain, some of her longing.

She swayed with the tenderness of his mouth as it moved over hers, the skill of his kiss making her feel light-headed and abandoned. The slow rhythm of his hands on her body echoed hers, smoothing over the soft cloth of his jacket, trailing around the contours of his big chest and resting briefly, wonderingly, where his heart hammered a tattoo as loud as hers.

He muttered in her mouth—French or patois, she wasn't sure, knowing only that his breath tantalised its sensitive interior so agonisingly that she willingly invited him to explore further. And when he did, and his tongue touched hers, she groaned aloud with the rawness of her own desire.

Her hair was loose now, tumbling on her shoulders, her eyes glistening and dazed. He kissed her throat, eased down her zip and let his teeth savage her pearly shoulders while his hands caressed her naked back.

It was wrong. She knew that. But knowing it didn't stop her. Something terrible was driving her—his mouth, his eyes, his murmurs of appreciation, the sheer animal hunger of his demands. And she couldn't, wouldn't, refuse.

The starvation had been too long, too deep. She'd found such pleasure in lovemaking before...but nothing like this!

Mandy threw her head back and moaned in her throat. The air touched her body with its warmth, caressing it. She was virtually naked now, her dress whispering to her feet. Blindly she kicked off her shoes and lifted her hands to Pascal's face, kissing him with deep passion, sobbing with need, frantic in her efforts to help him remove his jacket.

All she could hear was their laboured breathing. All she could see was his beautiful body, warm and hard, satin and steel. All she could feel was the tension coiled inside her and in him too, the terrible suppression of emotion and sexual need.

They were equal in their passion, clawing at one another, mouth on mouth, body thrust against body. They staggered across the soft, yielding sand, kissing and devouring as they went, their hunger rising with every step. And then, when soft grass met her feet, Mandy felt him bearing her down to the ground and they sank down together with a grunt of satisfaction.

His mouth was on every inch of her straining body, each kiss a torment of gently restrained passion. She too felt as though she wanted to touch the whole surface of his skin, to appease her own mouth where it had been so long starved of kissing. With a moan, she arched like a supple bridge as his tongue played with the rigid peaks of her breasts.

Suspended between pleasure and torture, she reached out to cradle his head, afraid and excited, all of her senses focused on the sensations raging inside her. It wasn't love and it wasn't wise. Opening her drugged eyes, she saw the deep, awed look of tormented bliss on his face and let out a husky cry.

He looked up at her with eyes so primeval, burning with such a shockingly sexual desire, that she moaned again, drawing him to her for a long, impassioned kiss. And she was sliding on his skin, her arms and legs tangling with his, the terrible ache inside her clamouring for satisfaction. Her hips ground into his and suddenly she felt a wonderful, velvet warmth inside her and she cried out aloud with the relief of it because it was so right: gentle enough not to hurt, yet hard and relentless enough to ease her hunger.

All the time they continued to kiss as though their mouths couldn't get enough of one another, his hands now holding her head tenderly, his athletic body driving deeper into hers while she—she who had never known such passion or responded so ardently and wantonly— wrapped her legs around his body and forced her heels into him, matching his rhythm, flying, flying...

The core of her body was melting, liquefying and enclosing him with ever tightening spasms. She cried out again and again, heard his hoarse whispers in her ears, the tension and the release lifting her to a moment of pure, soaring joy. And then she shuddered in his arms, felt the nerves in her skin quivering as she subsided, then lay supine and indolent beneath him while he gently kissed her neck, his breathing stertorous in her ear.

She hadn't realised she had slept. But she was woken by gentle kisses on her collarbone and drowsily she smiled because she felt wonderful.

'I want you,' husked Pascal.

'Tired,' she mumbled.

'You don't *have* to do anything,' he murmured in amusement.

But she did. After a short time he'd aroused her languid body so intensely with his sweetly agonising caresses that she had to move, to encourage him, to enjoy him again. This time it was less raw and pagan a love-making. This time...

She gave a little whimper of protest as Pascal coaxed her into a frenzy. This time it was a deeper and more powerful experience than anything she'd known with Dave.

And as she fought with Pascal, begged him to take her, used every wile to make him lose his new and infuriating control, a small part of her was saying, This is pure sex. Lust. And it shamed her because it was so utterly pleasurable and she couldn't get enough of Pascal's body. He felt the same about her. They sated themselves till dawn, inciting one another with touch and sight and sound and the scents of each other's body.

Then—and only then—did she push back the thought that it was more than lust. She knew because she felt complete in every way. In her body and her beautifully aroused and satiated senses, in her mind, her heart, her emotions. Something momentous had happened to her. Something that made her feel both afraid and elated.

And she felt rich for the first time in her life, finding an exhilaration in abandoning herself completely to the basic art of igniting the desires of an experienced and immensely strong-willed, powerful male and rendering him all but helpless by her touch.

The sense of power made her feel light-headed. And incredibly sexy. Incredibly fulfilled.

They swam naked, without breaking the silence between them. Words would have destroyed the timelessness, the spell that they had woven around each other.

With the glowing sky behind her she stood thigh-deep in the ocean and stretched her whole body without coyness, proud of the admiration in every line of Pascal's sultry mouth. And he was beautiful, his body perfect—

toned, tanned, with less white skin beneath his waist than there should have been, perhaps because he bathed nude sometimes, she imagined, here on this isolated beach.

The water slipped like silk around her body as she swam, and she thought that she must be more aware of every tiny sensation than at any time in her life. Her head lifted back to the gentle warmth of the sun's first rays and she floated on the water unselfconsciously, listening to the silver-throated birds.

Pascal's body came up beneath hers and she sighed. Some time one of them had to break the enchantment. She would become embarrassed and ashamed and they would have to accept that this had been the result of hunger and emotion, something never to be repeated. Her body contracted at the thought of the loss.

'Gently,' he murmured in her ear. He swam with her to the shallows, lifted her to her feet and drew her to him, kissing her with a brutal sweetness that made her want to cry. 'Relax,' he soothed, sucking on her lower lip. He smiled into her pained eyes. 'Take it easy.'

She didn't dare say why she was upset. Wickedly he nuzzled her ear and murmured his intentions while she tried to stop his hands from wandering all over her body, but he laughed and continued his bold exploration of each rib, each bone in her hips, the softness of her buttocks. 'Pascal!' she groaned, feeling her body reach meltdown as he lifted her into the air.

Slowly he brought her down and eased into her, watching her expression all the time. In despair she allowed her body to rule her mind again. It would be the last time, she promised herself. The very last time.

CHAPTER SEVEN

PASCAL'S leisurely caresses made Mandy feel beautifully languid, until a vibration that had an intensity she could hardly bear began to curl through her. There would never be anything like this again—only the misery and the terrible emptiness of her life would be left.

Together they climaxed with such abandon that they toppled over into the water, rolling instinctively to where the waves lapped their trembling bodies.

Pascal held her till she stopped sobbing, though when she'd begun to cry she didn't know, only recognising that now there was no more emotion left inside her. And then he picked her up, staggered, recovered himself, and took her across the beach to a small, open-sided summer house where he gently laid her on a bed and came to rest beside her, drawing up a soft linen sheet to cover them both.

She was dimly aware of someone murmuring outside, calling his name, and he drowsily muttered, *'Entrez!'* Mortified, Mandy hastily buried her head under the sheet. She heard the clatter of cups, his casual thanks and a soft reply. 'She's gone,' he said with lazy affection after a while. 'Want some breakfast?'

She lifted a hot and flushed face. 'Your staff don't seem surprised by what they see! How often do you do this?' she asked weakly, and thought how possessive she sounded. Her lower lip wobbled.

He kissed it gently and teased a strand of her rich brown hair. 'Only when I have to,' he said quietly.

Mandy gasped. She was one of many? That wonderful sex had been something repeated several times with other women? She wasn't special at all. And that realisation filled her with a searing, agonising pain. She went cold when the reason for that dawned. Somewhere along the line she'd mistaken lust for affection.

It had been different for her—a uniting of two people who shared common tragedies, who understood each other and had found solace and release in sharing themselves. For Pascal she was just a necessary outlet!

How many women? she wanted to ask, shaking with the vicious stabs that lanced through her. She was jealous! Worse than that; she was teetering on the brink of imagining that she'd been half in love. Ridiculous. But last night had been so perfect. Pascal had been a dream companion, a dream lover. Too good to be true.

'You brute!' she muttered miserably. 'I'm leaving! I'm going to find your father—'

With a quick curse under his breath Pascal gripped her wrist, his narrowed eyes searching hers. 'You can't go to him after me! Do you imagine he's any better than me in bed?'

'Pascal!' she cried in horror. 'You—you're crude, disgusting—!'

'You of all people can't call me names!' he roared, some terrible anguish racking him and making his voice crack. 'You were prepared to suck up to my father, crawl on your knees to him, *for* him—'

'Stop it! I might have said I was desperate, but not that desperate!' she yelled.

'So you'd have stuck to normal sex with him?' he snapped.

'No! I—'

'Perhaps a few tricks to amuse him?' he scathed.

Mandy felt paralysed, shocked beyond measure at what he was suggesting. He had it wrong. But she couldn't speak for her horror.

'Well, he's off the scene for a while, so you don't have much choice, do you? At least with me you'd be protected,' he snarled.

'Protected!' she gasped.

'Sure. With him you'd be ostracised. The staff at his house would serve you, but they would feel nothing but contempt for you. You say you like people. Living with my father would mean that you'd have to make do with the company of one ageing and dissipated man who is bitter and bad-tempered and hates the world and who's loathed in return—'

'Pascal! What are you saying?' she croaked.

'Forget my father. What guarantee do you have that he won't turn you out after a month or two, when your services are no longer required? You know you're not the first! Why do you think you might be the last? Plenty of others have been willing to lie in my father's bed—'

'Wait a minute!' she cried, grabbing Pascal's arms and shaking him frantically till he stopped his rasping tirade, her hair falling all around her face in a tumble of rich chestnut silk. She tossed it back angrily. 'What are you talking about?'

'All I know is that you asked me to take his place,' he said tightly, 'as your lover instead of him.'

'*What?*' she gasped hoarsely.

'I need...' he looked away from her luminous eyes '...sex. You provide it. And I keep you in comfort.'

Sex, she thought bleakly. That was what he'd arranged with her. A hot rush of shame washed through her. If he thought she'd willingly agreed to such a dreadful suggestion, no wonder he held her in contempt; no wonder his staff thought she was some cheap little tramp who wasn't worthy of their smiles.

'You've misunderstood what I meant,' she began in despair.

'No,' he said viciously. 'You won't play the innocent with me now. We've been too far for that. The minute I saw you I wanted you,' he growled. 'Even now every time I look at you I remember I'm a man, and I haven't felt like that for a long time. I need sex, Mandy. I don't want a relationship, only sex. And, to keep it exclusive, I'm willing to pay for it. Especially if it's always as wild as last night and this morning. But, if I keep you, you must stay away from other men—especially my father. Is that perfectly clear?'

'No!' Needing some kind of barrier between them, she drew the sheet up to her face, peering at him over the embroidered edge. 'There's been a genuine mistake—'

'He advertised for you,' he reminded her.

'Yes! So?' She raised her eyes to the ceiling, impatient that he should be so obtuse. 'I answered the advert which led me to a solicitor in London who said I wasn't to get my hopes up but I might be lucky. Obviously things don't always work out in these cases—'

Pascal grunted. 'You're right. Father didn't even see some of the women in the flesh. He'd wait for a photograph and the solicitor's assessment,' he said contemptuously. He looked down his nose at her, running his eyes over her body. 'And the best,' he said softly, 'he bought. Some very lovely women have passed through his hands.'

Mandy shook her head impatiently. 'You've got the wrong idea entirely!' she said hotly. 'He was helping those women! He wanted to help me! The last thing I want is to go to bed with your father! It's perfectly ridiculous, Pascal! I've never met the man! Besides, I won't ever get over Dave. Casual sex, a long-term relationship, love... they're all beyond my capabilities. My interest is dead,' she added in a shaky voice, suddenly, frighteningly, needing to convince herself.

These were the words she'd said so often to boyfriends. They'd become automatic. But this time they weren't true. Pascal had exploded her world of mourning and of clinging to the past. It would never be the same again.

'Last night?' he challenged. 'Wasn't that casual?'

She winced. How could he treat last night as if it had been casual? To her it felt momentous—a release of her suppressed sexuality, a miraculous fusing of two people in heart, mind and body. Deep within her she'd known with a woman's instinct that this could be the man for her. Of course she couldn't tell him so. But if she agreed that it hadn't been anything special, then he'd think that she'd indulged in casual sex! She couldn't win!

'I don't know how that happened,' she said honestly. 'I was emotional. I felt relieved that you were going to step into your father's shoes and help me! I've been hoping for so much, yearning to find someone here who cares about me! That's why I answered the advert, don't you see?' she cried passionately. 'I need someone of my own. Someone who can share my life. Companionship—'

'For God's sake!' he cried impatiently. 'Are you that naïve? Did he pull the wool over your eyes so easily? The other women who came here knew what was expected of them. Do you honestly think my father brought you over here and paid all that money so you could be his *friend*?'

'No! I'm *not* stupid! I know it was a business arrangement and—'

'You are the most cold-blooded of all the women he's ever taken on!' said Pascal contemptuously.

Mandy gulped. Did he mean the other women that Vincente St Honoré had helped in the past? Had the solicitor *really* demanded sexual favours for finding long-lost relatives? 'He hasn't bought me!' she protested shakily.

'He sent you air tickets—'

'Your father was only the intermediary,' she argued, 'acting on behalf of his client as any solicitor would.'

'Give me strength! My father's not a solicitor!' scoffed Pascal.

Mandy blinked, her eyes enormous. Her hands lowered
the sheet and she clutched at her thudding heart. 'Not...a
solicitor? Then...what is he?' she asked in confusion.

'A lecher. A spoiler of women,' grated Pascal. 'The
St Honorés don't take up professions. The land is our
life. Or it was, till Father decided sex was more fun.'

It was a moment before that sank in. And when it did
she stared at him mutely, her whole body frozen to ice
as the full implications began to reach her dulled mind.
'Then...the—the advert was...'

'For a mistress,' provided Pascal brutally, watching
her with an unnerving intentness.

'A—a...*mistress*! That can't be right!' she breathed.
'He—he knew my name and my birth date!' Her mouth
began to tremble at the thought that it might have been
a terrible mistake. 'He knew where I was born! It was
in the advert, along with my date of birth, the name of
the nursing home and the children's homes where I spent
my first eighteen years,' she cried, gaining confidence.
'That doesn't sound as if he's looking for a mistress,
does it? Pascal...your hatred of your father has led you
to misunderstand—'

'I have evidence,' he said coldly.

'So have I!' she countered. 'Mr Lacey handed me an
airline ticket to St Lucia, said my proof of identity was
in order and that I'd be contacted by Vincente St Honoré
and learn something to my advantage.'

'And what did you think that was?' he enquired, lifting
a disbelieving eyebrow.

'Surely you know? I thought you had all the details
of my case! I was expecting to make contact with my
parents!' she explained in exasperation.

Pascal's brows snapped together. 'Parents? What the
hell do you mean?'

'I thought...' She swallowed. 'I thought your father
was a solicitor, acting for someone in my family who'd
finally traced me,' she mumbled, pain beginning to

darken her eyes. 'I imagined that all the secrecy was connected with the fact that I could be illegitimate, a love-child of someone important—or perhaps married—and that it was a delicate matter to be handled carefully.

'Oh, Pascal,' she said plaintively, 'you must believe me! I thought I'd find my family! It's everything I've always wanted—that's why I came here! And—and I did so want to find out about my mother!' she finished jerkily.

He was very still, his chest rising and falling imperceptibly with his shallow breathing. 'Well, I'll be damned!' he muttered.

'I'd been searching for years,' she said unhappily, 'putting adverts in papers—'

'There you are,' he said gruffly. 'Father must have read one of them and decided you were a likely victim. Did you put in all the details about yourself, like your birth date and so on?' She nodded miserably. 'That's your explanation,' he growled. 'He used your own information to attract you. Defenceless, desperate women are his speciality.'

Her mind seemed to go dead. Pascal had found the solution. She'd been fooled in the cruellest way possible. Enticed by a lecherous old man halfway around the world, passed on to his equally sex-hungry son...

That she could cope with. But not with the fact that it had been a wild-goose chase. No relatives. Nobody to love, or to love her back unconditionally, no blood relation to share her life. Nothing but ashes in her mouth and a hole in her heart.

Cold shivers ran down her spine as she remembered with horror her earlier conversations with Pascal and realised that everything he'd said and done had been coloured by his belief that his father was in line to be her sugar-daddy. Now she knew what kind of woman he'd thought she was. A woman willing to share her body with an ageing man in return for a comfortable life.

A mail-order mistress.

She blinked away the tears which were beginning to form. Self-pity was a luxury she couldn't afford. She had to get out of this mess. 'I thought—I thought...' Bravely she rallied herself and tried to be optimistic. There could be a mix-up. Only meeting his father would reveal the truth. 'You could be wrong!' she said slowly, putting hope before logic. 'Maybe your father *does* know who my parents are—'

'I'm sorry, Mandy. I'd like to think so but it's highly unlikely,' Pascal said, sounding sympathetic. 'Father hasn't been off his plantation for the last thirty years—'

'Visitors?' she suggested in a small voice.

'None. His overseer keeps them at bay. He doesn't see anyone other than the women who come over from England or France to keep his bed warm for a fee.'

Grim-faced at the thought of his father's lifestyle, Pascal swung his legs off the bed and walked naked to the small table, pouring coffee for them both and handing her a cup before he settled on the bed again. His arm came around her and she was grateful for that. He evidently wasn't entirely driven by his sex urge.

'How does he meet these women if he doesn't ever leave his land?' she asked in a small voice.

'By advertising. I always suspected something like that was going on. When Father became ill and the overseer sent for me I sorted out the mass of correspondence and bills littering Father's desk.'

Feeling sick, she put down her cup. So did he. He drew her head onto his shoulder and left his hand to cradle her cold face while she slipped her arms around him and nestled closer for comfort.

'I found a file of newspaper cuttings advertising for female companions under the age of thirty,' he continued quietly. 'There was a request for details and photographs to be sent to a box number—and that, I discovered, was a cover for one of the partners in Lacey's firm.'

'But Lacey wasn't involved?' she cried in agitation.

'Probably not,' he answered, his mouth against her temple. 'Lacey's partner was dealing with my father's adverts for a companion. I found one dated only last month. When I read a copy letter to Lacey detailing Father's instructions about you, I jumped to the conclusion that you were the companion Father had chosen.' Gently he detached himself and looked deep into her eyes, which were swimming with unshed tears. 'You can see why.'

'Yes,' she said dully.

'Father asked me to meet you and take care of you till he was better. As far as I was concerned you were one of a long line of women who'd turned up on his doorstep.'

She cringed. 'I'm sure Mr Lacey knew nothing about this...soliciting of women. He's a nice man with a lovely family.'

'Trust you to know that!' said Pascal wryly.

'Well, I know he wouldn't have sent me out to St Lucia to be a kept woman! He—he honestly believed I was on my way to tracing my parents! It—it looks as if it was all a mix-up!' She winced in distress. 'There's no one here for me at all.'

He went silent. Eventually he said, as if in relief, 'You didn't know anything of this?'

'No.' Her voice was barely audible.

Pascal closed his eyes in pain and then looked at her with such tenderness that her heart skipped a beat. 'I'm sorry,' he said huskily. 'The St Honoré men have given you a tough time, one way or another.'

'It wasn't your fault,' she said woodenly, trying not to think of the impending journey back to England. 'You—you kept trying to warn me about your father,' she remembered with a sniff.

'Yes. He's always had mistresses. An old tradition handed on from father to son,' he said bitterly, 'from way back when we were French aristocrats and morals were different.'

'That's sickening!' she said in disgust. 'Marriage is sacrosanct.'

And she had to admit to herself that Pascal wasn't much better than his father. He'd been ready to take her on as his mistress too. Like father, like son.

Suddenly she moved away from Pascal. She needed to be on her own. She had to get used to that idea. Her time with Pascal had been nothing but a brief and intense holiday romance—and just as shallow.

'Come back,' he coaxed. 'Let me hold you. You must be so upset. Don't sit over there and shut me out.'

'Please,' she said, shaking her head. 'I need to come to terms with what's happened. It's such a shock.'

'I know. I remember what it was like when I found out Father was playing around,' he said grimly. 'Even at six years old I was aware of the gossip and my mother's shame when Father brought another woman into the house. My aunt says that Mother had known about his earlier infidelities. But this was something different—a deliberate insult to my mother's good name.' He frowned. 'I imagine she and Father had a row and that's when he hit her.'

Mandy's tender heart softened. 'Have you ever tried to trace her?' she asked gently.

He shook his head. 'When I grew older I thought about finding her,' he replied, 'but even if I could—and did—what then? She hated my father. She couldn't visit me without painful memories. I was afraid I'd ruin the new life she'd made, perhaps with another husband, a new family. She and Father were never divorced, you see. I could hurt her badly, just by satisfying my curiosity and some vague yearning.' Pascal's clear blue eyes blazed a message. 'I don't think it's wise to dwell on the past, Mandy.'

'You think I shouldn't pursue my dream?' she asked tentatively.

He smiled, and the sweetness of his mouth filled her with tenderness. 'That's for you to decide. But I'm glad you did or you wouldn't be here and last night would never have happened.'

Mandy sighed. She would never have known the beautiful island, never have discovered the extraordinary fires inside her or known that two people could create such joy. 'No,' she croaked, and her wistful glance lingered on him as she wished and wished that their union could have lasted more than just a brief moment in time.

Pascal reached out and pushed back the curtain of thick hair that had fallen over Mandy's face when she'd bent her head in regret. 'It was special, wasn't it?' he said softly.

'Mmm.'

'Mandy, I...' His hand fell away. 'I think I need something to eat,' he said unsteadily. 'I'm getting a little light-headed.'

He went over to collect the tray. When he brought it back it seemed to her that his eyes were melting with affection. Trembling a little, Mandy accepted the croissant he put on a plate for her.

'Thanks,' she mumbled.

He leaned over and kissed her gently on the lips. His palms came up to cup her face and he regarded her with a limpid warmth that made her heart lurch. 'I hate to think what would have happened to you if my father hadn't been taken ill. You would have been brought to his house as his next mistress. We would have met under very different circumstances.'

As if unable to bear that idea, he scowled and settled down beside her again, moodily picking up a warm croissant and tearing at it savagely with his teeth.

'Horrible!' She wrinkled her brow, trying to remember his words. 'You said something about encountering plenty of women, bright-eyed and hungry...'

His skin drawn tight over his cheekbones, he nodded grimly and said, 'They were always hopeful, looking for the wonderful life that money could buy. Usually I didn't meet the women till they were in trouble and desperate to leave. They'd come to me then and beg for money for their air fare home. Few put up with him for long.'

'How awful. I do feel sorry for them,' she said, her voice low and husky with compassion. 'It's a terrible way to live your life.'

'I feel sorry for anyone who tangles with my father.'

He passed her a jar of guava jam and Mandy suddenly thought how incongruous it was that they should be sitting up in bed eating breakfast like any married couple and discussing his father's mistresses.

'The ones who stayed...did he eventually dump them?' she asked tentatively.

'No. He hates change. I got rid of them by bribery,' Pascal said bluntly. 'Some I brought to Beau Jardin. I made them comfortable and did everything I could to talk them out of staying. Father was always threatening to bequeath Beau Rivage to whichever woman took his fancy the most. I couldn't bear to think of living next door to one of his ex-mistresses who worshipped money above decency. I did what I could to persuade the women to go.'

'Even keep them a prisoner.'

'Once. The others accepted money and air tickets home.'

'Did you provide them with a moonlit dinner by the sea?'

He shifted uncomfortably. 'Only one before you.'

And Mandy felt the breath shuddering out of her. 'And did this other woman resist the little stroll along the beach afterwards?' she asked huskily.

'I never offered. I never wanted any of them. They'd been with my father, don't forget,' he said in disdain.

'And...if I had been with him?'

Pascal recoiled, his eyes telling her that he couldn't countenance that idea. 'It doesn't bear thinking about,' he growled.

'Why did you make love to me, Pascal?' She knew what she wanted him to say. And knew that he'd disappoint her. But she had to ask.

'You know why. We needed each other.'

Although he said no more, his mouth had softened, causing her body to shimmy as if he'd caressed it. But she remembered that he'd told her he needed sex without strings. Pascal deplored his father's habit of acquiring mistresses, but he had the same cavalier attitude towards women.

She closed her eyes, squeezing them tightly, blotting out her need for him. It was only a substitute for the love she wanted from her own family. She felt Pascal remove the plate from her lap and lean over to put the tray on the side-table. A long silence fell.

That was it, then. The end of her hopes. Nothing was left. 'Will you take me back to the hotel?' she asked listlessly, opening her eyes at last. She felt dead. The future seemed dark and dreary.

'If that's what you want. You intend to go home on the eighteenth?' he asked gently. Her lip trembled and then her chin wobbled too. 'Mandy!' he sighed, gathering her in his arms and rocking her. 'You fool. You fool.'

'I can't help it! I'm so miserable! I'll be all—all right in—a—minute,' she said jerkily, her voice muffled by his chest. 'I've got to come to terms with not finding m-my family,' she wailed. 'Oh, hell!'

His hand stroked her shining hair soothingly. 'Hush. Hush,' he whispered.

'I arrived with such hopes,' she mumbled.

'I know,' he said fondly. 'I remember the way you looked when you came down the hotel steps—like someone who'd been set alight. God! I could *kill* my father for hurting you!' he growled savagely.

She put her arms around his neck and laid her head on his shoulder. It was nice. She felt protected. 'I'll keep trying to trace them when I get home,' she whispered. Pascal murmured something comforting, his mouth on her temple. Being hugged was lovely. She didn't want to emerge from his arms for a long time. 'Dave and I invented wonderful mothers for ourselves,' she reminisced, with a rueful smile. 'They were the best cooks, the best dressmakers and the highest-paid businesswomen in the world!'

'Of course!' Pascal chuckled, his breath warming her scalp, and she hugged him tightly.

'Our fathers were tall and handsome and dignified,' she continued dreamily, 'and worked in one of the caring professions. Dave's was a philanthropist who owned beautiful homes for the elderly; I favoured a paediatrician!'

Pascal brushed his lips over her forehead. 'The perfect family,' he murmured.

'I know it was foolish,' Mandy admitted, 'and we didn't expect anything like that. Normal parents with faults would have been fine,' she sighed wistfully. 'Knowing my luck, I'll discover that my mother is a weather-beaten navvy and my father lives under Battersea Bridge.'

'I'd offer you my father if I didn't like you so much,' said Pascal drily.

She detached herself from him and smiled. 'That's nice,' she said, solemn-eyed. 'Thank you.'

He hesitated, his lips parting. And hers did too. His lashes fluttered down. Mandy knew that he was going to kiss her—a proper kiss—and she waited, excitement building up inside her. Nothing sexual. Just an overwhelming delight and a deep desire to be touched by him.

When their lips met she sighed in her throat and slid her fingers into his fair curls. He was about to draw away but she prolonged the kiss, suddenly panicking. She'd never see him again. They had no reason to be together. 'Oh, Pascal!' she said brokenly when he thrust her back.

'I can't let you go,' he said roughly.

'Pascal,' she said, startled. 'I—'

'Listen. I've got to say this. You'll think I'm like my father but I'm not. I swear I'm not. I've done everything I could *not* to grow up like him. Any similarities I detected were ruthlessly expunged. You've got to listen to me. Don't interrupt. Will you do that?'

'All right,' she said uncertainly, bewildered by his intense expression.

'My wife died nearly ten years ago,' he said quickly, hurriedly, as if he had something urgent to tell her. 'She was nineteen when we married and I adored her. I know how you feel about your late husband. I felt like that about Caroline. She was all I had, the only female love—other than my aunt's—that I'd ever known. When she died with my baby son my world ended. Being in prison didn't even matter.'

He frowned, clearly trying to control his emotions, and Mandy's heart melted in the face of his heartache. 'I tried to forget her. I took off my wedding ring to break the hold she had over me. It didn't work. I believed then that I'd never know love like that again,' he said huskily, 'and so I shut women out of my life.'

'I understand,' she said quietly.

Pascal held her firmly by the shoulders and fixed her with his sea-deep eyes. 'And then you came along. Last night...' he said softly. 'Last night was something extraordinary for me. I've been celibate for so long, hungry for so long, wishing I could release my physical feelings. But I didn't want to pretend to a woman that I wanted to start an emotional relationship.'

'I—I understand that,' she admitted. Sorrow filled her misty eyes. 'It was nice to be held. To sleep in caring arms again.'

'Yes,' he muttered, his warm breath caressing her face. 'To know the pleasure of being touched. To smell a woman's scent, to stroke her skin, to feel the softness of her body... Sex,' he said bitterly. 'My curse is to have my father's urges with none of his immorality. I don't want to be tied emotionally and yet I need a woman in my life. I don't want to pretend to any woman that I'm capable of falling in love, because I'm not.'

Tenderly he kissed Mandy's parted lips and groaned into them. She shuddered, wrapping her arms around his body. 'A dilemma,' she whispered.

'Mmm.' He smiled, his eyes warm. 'We're so alike,' he murmured. 'Alone, with the same kind of past that we can't forget. Mandy...' He paused, struggling with some question that he felt unable to ask. She waited, her eyes telling him to speak, and he drew in a breath and said, 'Stay.'

Stunned, she stared at him uncomprehendingly. But she couldn't prevent her involuntary delight from showing in her face, or the longing that made her body tense with hope. 'I am staying,' she said shakily. 'Till the eighteenth.'

'And then?'

She bit her lip, knowing that she wanted to delay returning to her empty life—and knowing too that such a decision would only end in sorrow. Her face set in stiff lines. 'I go home.'

'I want to spend time with you. More than a week or so,' murmured Pascal, his velvety voice melting her resolve. 'We need each other, Mandy. We have a world in common and you can't deny that the chemistry between us is spectacular. Last night proved that.'

'I'm not promiscuous.' Her solemn eyes dared him to say otherwise. 'Dave was the only man who'd ever made love to me.'

'I know and I feel honoured,' Pascal said gently. His mouth drifted over her forehead, her cheekbone, her throat. He murmured persuasively into the warm hollow where her pulse throbbed with a faltering beat, 'Stay with me. We'll take it one step at a time. No demands, no expectations. Just the warmth that we feel for each other. Both of us have been hurt. You especially. We deserve something good in our lives, don't we?'

He smiled at her with such affection that she felt her heart lurch with longing. If only he loved her. If only she loved him. It would be so wonderful. But too good to be true.

'I can't—'

'Or won't? Or are you afraid of being hurt? Don't you think that scares the hell out of me too?' he asked wryly. 'But I trust you because you're gentle and kind and you wouldn't intentionally kick me in the teeth, would you?' She shook her head. 'No. And don't you know in your heart of hearts that I'd never hurt you?'

'Mmm.' It was all she could manage. It was so tempting. But utterly against everything she'd ever held dear: her honour, her self-respect—and the respect of others. If she loved a man enough then she expected him to court her and marry her, not invite her to sleep with him as a cheap and more disposable alternative to a lifetime partner.

'I know you want to stay,' he said throatily.

'I'm not prepared to have a casual relationship,' she said flatly, her voice betraying her regret. And although she did not know it her face showed how torn she was and what an effort it cost her to refuse him. She was close to tears again. Pascal's embrace was so tender, so loving and she wanted to remain in the protection of his arms. 'I could never face myself in the morning,' she muttered. 'I'm not that sort.'

'Spend the day with me. Defer your decision till later,' he suggested.

And because she wanted to be held by him she nodded her head. But she knew what her answer would be.

For a while they lay together, thinking their own thoughts and listening to the bird song, the rustle of the palm leaves and the soft roll of the surf on the beach. Unhurriedly, they then showered and dressed, and walked for miles—first along the dramatic, wave-cut coastline, up and down the cliffs and inlets, and then back through the beautifully kept acres of pineapple fields, mango and cashew-nut trees.

That day turned into another. And another. Neither of them wanted to say the words which would end their time together.

At the end of a week Mandy knew that she had fallen deeply in love with Pascal. And it almost broke her heart when she told him that she would leave later that day because she could see their relationship drifting on with no commitment on his part and she had to go home and live in the real world.

Arm in arm, they wandered in the exuberant gardens where purple-throated and crested hummingbirds hovered in the trumpets of outsize hibiscus and the fluffy puffball trees. He tucked fragrant frangipani flowers in her hair and kissed her so sweetly that she almost cried.

'It's all right,' he said, when she became more and more tense as the afternoon light began to fade. 'I won't bully you. I don't want to hurt you, you see. But I want to be with you, Mandy. I care about you.'

'Don't!' In distress, she wrenched herself away and stood forlornly looking out to sea. The sun was setting. It hung like a huge, glowing orange low in the sky, and soon it would dip to the horizon and then it would be gone and the night would descend. Black and uncom-

promising. And she'd have to take the boat back to the
hotel before dark. 'I can't bear it!' she whispered.

'You can't bear what? To be alone again?'

She didn't respond. How could she tell him that—
after such a short time—she knew that they could be
happy for ever? But they'd been together constantly,
night and day, waking and sleeping. They'd spent more
time with each other than many couples did before becoming engaged.

And she knew that they were right for one another
with a certainty that was all the more poignant because
she could not possibly voice it now. Too soon. Men didn't
have that intuition, did they? He'd think that she was
trying to push him into a deeper commitment and that
she was seeking financial security after all.

'I think we'd better not see each other again,' she
croaked.

Pascal groaned and took a step towards her, then
somehow stopped himself although she knew that he was
as unhappy as she about the parting. Yet he was refusing to set his heart free. He seemed sure that he only
wanted someone for sex and to ease his loneliness.
Whereas she had love to give. Now. It overwhelmed her
at that moment, perhaps because their separation was
so close, and she began to shake.

To disguise her weakness, she sank to the grass and
pretended to be waiting for the sunset. But she clenched
her fists till her knuckle-bones stood out hard and white
and as raw as her emotions.

'Mandy,' he said helplessly.

The sorrow in his voice made her turn her head away
because his misery was too much for her. He needed her.
That was evident in the way they held one another after
making love, in their happiness together, the close friends
they'd become. Everything in her nature balked against
walking away from him.

'Don't ask it,' she begged shakily, barely audible. 'You're asking for more than I'm prepared to give.'

In an electric silence they watched the sun sinking, closer and closer to the hard-edged horizon. Its lower rim began to disappear while the sky blazed scarlet and purple.

As if driven, Pascal said roughly, 'If you're leaving, you must go in a few moments.'

'I know!' Her hand lifted helplessly and fell again, and she pressed it to the ground as if she might anchor herself there.

'Time is running out for us.'

'Please!' she wailed.

Then she felt her chin being tipped up and Pascal's satiny mouth on hers, his tongue stroking along the trembling fullness of her upper lip. 'I won't let you! We have to be together!' he breathed. Warm and welcome, his arms enclosed her and she was his willing prisoner. 'I don't care how. I'll make a commitment if that's what you want. Love isn't something I can give...yet. I'm still hurting, Mandy. I still think of Caroline and Charles too much, too often. But I do care about you.'

'You do?' she asked shakily.

He smiled. 'Yes, I do. I can give you a comfortable life, a companion, someone to share those special moments with. I can give you a kind of happiness that we might not find elsewhere. We can both give each other incredible sexual satisfaction. That alone is something rare.' He touched her hair wonderingly and Mandy's heart lurched at his tenderness. 'I want you to marry me, Mandy. It seems the only solution.'

'Marriage? Marriage!' There was a sudden rush of warmth enveloping her, a surge of great emotion that cut all sense from her brain. Marriage. It would be wonderful. But she loved him. How long before he accepted that he might be falling in love with her? She bit her lip and looked down, her lashes fluttering heavily on her cheeks. 'I—I don't know...'

'I think you do,' Pascal said gravely. 'We've both known it from that moment when I first held you in my arms. Look at me!' he ordered. She did so, reluctantly, knowing that she'd be taken captive by his eyes. 'I will promise you two things,' he said huskily. 'To remain faithful to you, and to trace your family. One way or another I'll do that for you, even if I have to travel the world to do so.'

'Oh, Pascal!' she cried, choking with emotion. He cared that much. Her eyes softened with love. 'It's all I've ever wanted!' Pascal and her family! The joy made her face radiant and then a shadow crossed it. Dared she risk something so precious as her heart in a marriage with a man who openly admitted that he wasn't in love? Maybe he'd never love her. Maybe he'd never forget Caroline...

He took away all her doubts by kissing her. Gently, hungrily, desperately. And while his ruthless, searching mouth plundered hers she couldn't keep her rationality intact. His ardour tugged at her heartstrings cruelly. With him she could forget everything. Even her senses.

'Hold me, Mandy,' he groaned hoarsely. 'Hold me. I need you!'

'I need you,' she said, bewildered by her defence-lessness against his passion.

'Then you'll say yes,' he persisted, his fierce gaze melting into her.

It was a foregone conclusion. Of course she'd marry him. And trust to fate. 'Yes,' she whispered helplessly, afraid even as she said the word. 'Yes!'

CHAPTER EIGHT

FIVE days later Mandy was married on the hotel beach at sunset, beneath a bower of orchids and lilies. Still dazed. Still unable to unwind her mind from its muddled state because Pascal had flung her into a round of meetings and arrangements, flying her to Barbados to buy her wedding dress, choosing the food for the banquet, colour schemes for the flowers, the cake, guest lists...

She'd barely had time to breathe, let alone think. But when she had—usually when she was soaking in the bath—she'd felt scared—oh, so scared—fretting that she'd been stupid—which was true—but knowing that she couldn't bear the thought of leaving Pascal. He was everything she could wish for: attentive, courteous, kind and very, very loving.

As the days had rolled on she'd seen how well he managed his staff and how much they respected him and referred to him with affection. They seemed to like her too, and she felt sure that, in time, the people at the hotel would realise that she had been the victim of a misunderstanding.

Pascal would be good to her, she knew that. But marriage was a huge step. And she was taking it so quickly that it tended to unnerve her till he held her again in his arms, and then all her fears flew out of the window. The fears came back again, however, whenever they were parted, and had done especially when she'd spoken to her superior on the phone and meekly agreed that she was crazy, but asked if he'd say goodbye to the people on her round for her.

Sometimes, curled up on the big sofa with Pascal in the evenings, talking about their plans, she'd felt as if it was all a dream and it was impossible that she could be so happy.

And now the impossible was coming true. She was wearing an alarmingly expensive designer-label wedding dress and holding Pascal's hand while he thanked all the guests, staff and fascinated holiday-makers for celebrating his wedding to 'the most beautiful woman I have ever seen'.

It was a lovely compliment and it brought a shy smile to her face. But it was the dress which gave her the illusion of beauty, with its soft peach shading, the long, flowing skirt and sweetheart neckline. And the bodice fitted so snugly to her ribs and waist that it emphasised the soft swell of her breasts and hips in the most flattering way. She felt gorgeous, and with Pascal's melting gaze on her she basked in his frank admiration.

'Thank you!' she murmured, her shining eyes fixed on his.

He put his hand on her flowing hair and, careful of the orchids twined in it, he gently kissed her. 'Thank *you*,' he said softly. His smile took her breath away and she sighed happily.

Somewhere to her left a woman sniffed. Startled, she looked up, to see his unmarried aunt Susannah, overcome with emotion. Mandy abandoned Pascal and ran to Susannah, catching her hands warmly. 'Don't cry! We are happy,' she said in reassurance. 'I know what Pascal means to you. I'll make him happy.'

'I know! I know he loves you!' Susannah smiled through her tears, clutching her tightly, and Mandy wished that it were so.

On the few occasions when Susannah had left her apartments in the big house and spent the evening with them, she had teased Pascal because everyone had been saying that he talked of nothing but his bride-to-be.

Mandy had felt a wrench of unease that he was fooling
people so ably. And a slight tremor of fear had run
through her when she'd thought of his skill at deception. But she'd told herself that he was only trying
to hide the truth—that he was marrying because she'd
safely fulfil his physical needs.

Mandy felt a deep affection for Susannah, perhaps
because she looked so like Pascal with her curly fair hair
and blue eyes, and because Susannah evidently adored
him. So, for his aunt's sake, Mandy kept up the pretence
that she and Pascal loved one another. Maybe it would
be mutual one day. It was her secret hope and she hugged
that idea to herself every night before she fell asleep.

'We'll only be gone for a few weeks,' she said encouragingly as Susannah blew into her handkerchief.
'Then we'll be together as a family.'

His aunt howled in response to that remark. Pascal
came and put his arms around the two women, laughing
them out of their tears. 'The boat's waiting,' he said
lovingly. 'Take care, Susannah.'

'You're... you're like a son to me,' mumbled his distraught aunt.

'I know. You were a good mother to me when I needed
one. But I'm a bit old to be your son, Susannah!' he
laughed. 'There's hardly sixteen years between us! Cheer
up,' he said affectionately. 'And let me know if my
father's condition deteriorates,' he added, frowning as
he took off his shoes and socks and rolled up his trouser-
legs ready to wade through the surf. 'Don't tell him I'm
married yet. I need to do that in my own time.'

'I wouldn't tell him,' said Susannah fervently. 'Not in
a million years.'

'Are you taking me on honeymoon or not?' protested
Mandy, and he laughed, sweeping her up into his arms.
'I'm only teasing. Your aunt adores you,' she said gently.

'I know. I'm all she has and she fusses over me as if
she were my real mother!' he answered wryly.

He strode through the surf to the waiting pirogue and placed her gently on the wide wooden seat before joining her. With the boatman singing a soft, Creole boat-song in the background, they made the short journey to his motor yacht, moored a little way offshore.

Beneath the stars that night they ate a wedding barbecue on deck, some twenty miles to the south of St Lucia. Mandy lay on the lounger on deck, watching the surf wash the beach of a deserted island a few yards away, and thought that she'd never been so happy in all her life. Pascal was kind. The crew adored him. He'd charmed everyone at the wedding and had made it a day to remember all her life.

'Penny,' he said gently.

'I was thinking how deceptive first impressions can be,' she said with a laugh. 'You pretended to be hard and cold. You're about as hard and cold as cooked dasheen!'

His grin gleamed white in the half-dark. 'You're taking to island life like a duck to water,' he said in approval. 'Cooked dasheen, indeed! I can be hard and ruthless when I have to. Wait and see.'

'Is that a threat?' she giggled.

'Definitely,' he growled. 'Come here. I want to see if you taste different now you're a married woman.'

Mandy happily surrendered to his arms, giving her entire heart and body to him, till she thought that she must pay for such happiness in some terrible way. No one could be as blissful as she and not pay a price.

But they grew closer, becoming greater friends and more adventurous lovers over the next three weeks as they cruised around the Grenadines, laughing more together than she would have thought possible. She told him about herself, about her happy life with Dave. But he wouldn't speak much about his own background and she knew that it hurt him still to think of it.

Their homecoming was an excuse for a vast party, given by his aunt, with the plantation house decked in flowers and steel bands playing on the beach. That night they went to the panelled master bedroom, in a part of the house Mandy hadn't seen before. Tenderly he undressed her and tenderly they made love in the big bed draped in pure linen and lace. Mandy felt as if her heart would break if she didn't tell him soon how she felt.

'I'm going to see Vincente,' announced Susannah the next morning. 'Shall I tell him you'll be visiting in the near future, Pascal?'

He made a face and quartered a slice of mango before answering. 'I suppose I'll have to,' he said shortly. 'I must check on his mail too. Not today, though. Mandy wants to see Herbert, the minibus driver. She said she promised to visit. We'll do that today. I'll call in on Beau Rivage tomorrow morning then go to the hospital in the afternoon.'

Mandy could sense his tension all through the boat journey to Soufrière, where Herbert lived. And when they set off in the taxi he'd hailed she tried to jolly him out of his mood because it hurt her when he was sad.

'It's very picturesque,' she said, admiring the faded elegance of the sun-bleached, wooden buildings in the old French fishing town. Many houses had verandas which were decorated with elaborate fretwork carvings, as if someone had been at work with an icing set.

'It used to be the capital of St Lucia before they developed Castries in the north,' he said idly. 'The Empress Josephine played as a child at Mal Maison, not far from here.'

'Such glamour,' she sighed. 'I can imagine it all. The parties, the flirting...'

'We still know how to party,' he answered with a grin. 'I met Caroline at a smart version of the local jump-up.'

Mandy nodded. He'd promised to take her to one of the Friday-night jump-ups. Friday night, Saturday

morning, loud music and dancing in the streets, hot food
from street vendors... She suddenly realised that he'd
mentioned his late wife and she might find out something about his past.

'What was she like?' she asked tentatively. 'There
aren't any photographs of her around.'

A shadow fell on his face. 'They were all burnt in the
fire,' he answered heavily, and she reached out to cover
his hand with hers in sympathy. 'Our house was further
up the track from Beau Rivage. I designed and built it
myself, with the help of the plantation carpenter. Nothing
remains of it. The jungle has covered it all.'

'I can't bear to think of it!' she said, clasping her hands
together passionately.

'Well—' he tensed his jaw '—you know how it is.
You've been there too. I never said goodbye; that was
the worst of it. I'd gone for an early-morning ride and
had crept out of bed so as not to wake Caroline.'

'I suppose there's no doubt that it was your father
who caused the fire?' she suggested hesitantly.

It made her heart go out to him to see him trying to
control his emotions by unnecessarily smoothing the
crease in his beige linen suit.

'Susannah saw him by my house, smoking one of his
cigars. Father denied being there at all. But I'd rather
believe Susannah. Why would she lie about something
like that? I saw the smoke from a distance and rode like
hell, but when I arrived the house was a ruin.'

'And then?' she asked quietly.

He stared gloomily out of the window. 'I went berserk
and dragged Father out of his study and threw him into
the garden. His men hauled me off, otherwise God knows
what I might have done to him. Caroline and Charles
were everything to me and I'd lost them because one
stupid old man couldn't be bothered to put out his damn
cigar properly. Father then made a complaint to the

police. He destroyed our family,' he said bitterly. 'And Caroline's too. They've never forgiven me for her death.'

'But it wasn't your fault!' she cried, upset.

'As far as they're concerned, if I hadn't married Caroline she'd still be alive,' he muttered. 'That's how they see it. I wasn't flavour of the month when we married.'

'Why?' she asked indignantly.

He shrugged. 'Father's behaviour was notorious and they were afraid I'd inherited all his worst traits. I can't blame the Cavendish family for wanting their daughter to marry someone else. We were an odd lot. Father had brought his mistress into the house after countless affairs, he'd ostracised Louis, his own cousin, to the extent that they strode up and down their borders with loaded shotguns, and he'd bullied and subdued Susannah, his own sister, so thoroughly that she became a permanent spinster.'

'But you were so much in love that you defied everyone and married,' she prompted, wondering if she'd ever find anything at all to like about his father.

'We had to.' He turned to face her. 'Caroline became pregnant,' he said gently. 'It was a deliberate act on our part, to force the Cavendish family to see that our marriage was inevitable—and we both wanted a child very much.'

'But they never accepted you? Didn't they see how good you were and how much you loved Caroline?' she asked heatedly. 'Surely they could tell you were kind and hard-working and—'

'Spare me the flattery,' he said with a rueful laugh. 'There was a little more to it than that. They were English settlers from way back. They thought they could do better for their daughter than me.'

'That's ridiculous!' she said stoutly. 'But... are you saying that her family live on St Lucia?'

'There's only her younger brother left now. He has a plantation on the edge of the rainforest.'

'You should have told me!' exclaimed Mandy. 'Weddings are a good time to heal old wounds. We should have asked him to the wedding—'

'You have a kind heart, Mandy,' he said, leaning over and kissing her protesting mouth. 'But Jake Cavendish would never have come. Besides, he's something of an absentee owner. He's a Reuter's war correspondent and spends most of his time abroad.'

'I think someone ought to tell him you're blameless,' she said crossly. 'And worth a million other men.'

He grinned. 'Thank you. I doubt Cavendish would agree. All I wanted to do was to run the plantation, and that wasn't good enough for his family. They'd imagined some whizkid from the high echelons of English society as their son-in-law, not a French rogue with a Caribbean accent!' he said with a rueful chuckle.

She beamed. 'I love your accent,' she confided. 'I want one!'

'Get educated in the University of the West Indies,' he said, 'and it's free.'

'No expensive Paris schools?' she teased.

'I was educated in England for a while,' he said surprisingly. 'In the banana trade you need good English. It's mandatory. But I missed home and I was going to have to be away for five years. I was desperately homesick for St Lucia and I ran away. Father was furious. He sent me to our Belgian château and I attended a college for the sons of gentlemen for a while.' Mandy's eyes widened. A Belgian château! 'I finally ended up where I wanted to be,' continued Pascal, 'spending university terms in Barbados and coming home for odd weekends and holidays. Wonderful.'

'Yes,' she said fondly. 'It is.'

'I think,' he said, almost to himself, 'that I would take the law into my own hands if anyone ever tried to take away my inheritance. My dream is to link Beau Rivage and Beau Jardin and all the rest of the St Honoré wealth again.'

And she felt the same. Perhaps through their children the St Honoré estates would cease to be hostile areas of contention where—so Pascal's overseer told her—the workers had to be careful to note the imaginary boundary lines between the flame-trees if they didn't want Vincente St Honoré firing buckshot at them.

'That's Herbert's house,' he said suddenly.

'And look!' she cried in excitement. 'There's Herbert!'

She jumped out of the taxi the moment it stopped and ran over, delighted to see that his whole family was lined up on the veranda, waiting for her.

After being shown around the tiny house, with Mandy wondering where on earth everyone slept, they went outside to the small garden to drink freshly squeezed lime juice beneath a tall, flowering immortelle tree which had scattered its red blooms all over the ground. Pascal and Herbert talked earnestly about the banana trade and the search for new markets while she played with the children and ate banana chips.

'Mr St Honoré,' said Herbert's sweet-faced wife, 'he's real happy! I never did see him so happy. He loves you, Mandy. And look—see how he holds my baby? Soon he'll want babies of his own.'

Wide-eyed, Mandy watched Pascal. He was lifting the baby into the air in an age-old game that fathers loved the world over. Her heart ached to see him, knowing that he must have played the game with his own son. And she wondered if she did already carry his child. She knew it was a possibility. At the thought of a baby her face suffused with an unspeakable joy.

'I would love to be a mother,' she said softly.

'You got that look about you, girl!' crowed Herbert's wife.

Pascal sensed Mandy's intense gaze, turned sharply and grinned broadly at her. 'Herbert's going to pollinate the orchids. Want to come and see?' he called.

Mandy giggled with Herbert's wife at the connection between their conversation and pollination and jumped up eagerly. She ran to Pascal, laughing when the baby chortled merrily as he swung the child onto his shoulder and began to bounce along. 'Pascal,' she said, unable to keep her feelings a secret any longer. 'Pascal...' She sighed. He looked at her with such tenderness...surely Herbert's wife had been right? If it wasn't love, then it was a deep affection. And that would be enough. 'Pascal,' she said softly, 'I love you.'

The smile left his face. His eyes closed and for one terrible moment she thought that he was going to be angry with her for spoiling their agreement. Then he lifted the baby down and held him out with a silent but commanding look at one of the older children, who took the little boy away.

Gently he took Mandy in his arms. 'And I you,' he said huskily. They stared and smiled at one another idiotically till the children tugged Mandy's skirt and demanded that she watch their father.

Lost in a magical world, she tried to concentrate while Herbert explained how he was hand-pollinating the vanilla orchids growing on the cocoa tree to encourage the vanilla pods to form. But she was only conscious of Pascal's warm body against hers, the rapid beat of her heart and the growing feeling that she carried their child. He loved her. He really loved her!

Herbert's wife was laughing behind them. 'I think you two got something to talk about!' she cried in glee. 'Herbert! They not listening to you! Get the bus out the shed and take Mr St Honoré back to the harbour,' she ordered, beaming all over her broad face.

Mandy blushed at Pascal's amused raised eyebrow. 'I think we should go,' she said, embarrassed. 'But we'll call again, Herbert.'

The children affectionately hugged them both. Pascal was wonderful with them, she thought dazedly as they drove back to Soufrière Bay. Maybe she and Pascal hadn't had much luck with their own parents, but they'd start a new family and give their children love and security. And someday, she mused dreamily, perhaps Pascal's efforts to trace her background through a network of detective agencies would bear fruit.

'Something to tell me?' he asked when they were alone on the boat.

She watched the crew cheerfully preparing to cast off from the jetty. Drawing in a huge breath, she scanned the wide alluvial valley and the low buildings of Soufrière nestled at the foot of the incomparable Pitons. 'Are you happy?' she asked.

'More than I could ever have imagined,' he answered in a voice low with choking emotions. He kissed her hands. 'I thought once that I would never stop loving and mourning Caroline. I believed there would be no one who could take away the pain and the sense of being abandoned by everything good and wonderful. You see, I thought you could only fall in love once.'

'Perhaps that's true,' she said, her lashes spiky with happy tears. 'What I feel for you is deeper than my feelings for Dave.'

Pascal's eyes kindled. 'My darling!' he said softly. 'I think maybe you're right. It's hard to recall my feelings for Caroline now; they're only a pleasant memory. I won't ever forget her, Mandy, but what we have seems to be on a different plane.'

'Everything you've said goes for me too,' she told him lovingly. 'As far as I was concerned Dave was the beginning and the end of my love life. I think maybe he opened my heart and I was the one who closed it. You've given me something I can't express properly; I only know that I feel ours is a love that will survive anything—and I haven't dared to risk saying so before. Now I don't care.'

'Mandy! I love you!' He kissed her tenderly, lingeringly. 'I have everything I could ever want—'

'Everything?' she asked breathily, arching a dark brow. And her eyes asked if he wanted their child.

He stiffened with surprise, gave a half-laugh and then his mouth was serious and laughing at the same time, his eyes somehow hopeful and wary.

'Do you mean—?' It was obvious that he hardly dared ask.

'I'm not sure,' she said demurely. 'I'm only ten days late and—'

'Mandy!' He crushed her in a bear-hug and then jerked away. 'Hell! I mustn't do that!' he cried, and she laughed at him. 'OK. You're not that delicate. I know—don't laugh at me! I'm only a man! But...Mandy, this is wonderful! I couldn't be any happier,' he said gruffly. 'When? How do you feel? Is the heat too much?'

'I'm fine,' she said blissfully. 'If I *am* pregnant, then it'll be *ages* yet. November-Decemberish. I haven't even risked fate by looking at dates. You must tell your father we're married,' she added in gentle reproach. 'And maybe, when we're sure I'm pregnant and he knows he's going to be a grandfather, you and he can be reconciled. That would be lovely, wouldn't it? People change, Pascal.'

'I wonder,' he muttered, sounding reluctant. 'I wonder. All right. I'll tell him. He won't be pleased, though.'

'Why?' she asked, puzzled. 'I've never understood why you've kept our marriage a secret. You insist that you're not ashamed of me and yet—'

'Of course I'm not!' he retorted. 'It's just that Father was furious when he knew Caroline was pregnant. I don't know what his problem is. It's as if he doesn't want me to inherit or to have an heir. And that hurts.'

'But...you're his lawful son!' she cried.

'I might as well not be,' Pascal said bleakly. 'He's never treated me with an ounce of affection or shown any pride in what I've achieved. I told you he's threatened several times to leave his money and the land elsewhere. God knows why. It's a personal affront to him that I've made a success of my plantation.'

'He must be a very lonely, unhappy man,' mused Mandy.

Pascal scowled. 'It's all his own doing.' Then he brightened. 'When we get back,' he said fondly, 'we'll get Anseydit—the carpenter—to come with us into the jungle and choose a tree for the baby's cradle—'

'Hey!' laughed Mandy. 'I'm not *sure* yet, Pascal!'

He smiled at her and held her close.

And after a little while she had confirmation. She carried his child.

It was nearly three weeks before Pascal left to visit his father. There had been trouble with the engine on the motor yacht and it was laid up in Marigot Bay for repairs. A section of the road was blocked again, and because several of his men were sick with a virus that was sweeping the local villages Pascal had been working feverishly with his reduced staff, trying to clear it to make it easier for the packers to bring the hands of bananas down from the upper valley.

But Mandy was deliriously happy and so was Pascal. She and Susannah discussed babies with a remarkable enthusiasm on Susannah's part, and Mandy felt touched that Pascal's aunt should take such an interest.

By dinnertime Pascal hadn't returned. She imagined that he'd met someone and her mood was so calm that she didn't worry, even when she went to bed at one o'clock in the morning and he still hadn't come back.

But when the next day dawned her heart missed a beat as she woke to find that he wasn't beside her.

'Susannah!' she yelled, racing recklessly over the polished mahogany floor of the sitting room to where Susannah sat on the deck of her apartment eating breakfast. 'Have you seen Pascal? He didn't come home last night!'

'No.' Susannah was busy packing mango jam into her pancake. Her hands seemed shaky and she dropped a dollop of jam on the tablecloth, laboriously concentrating on scraping it up and not meeting Mandy's eyes.

Mandy felt a little foolish since Pascal's aunt didn't find his absence worrying. Frowning, she fiddled with the ribbon on her lace peignoir. 'Where will he have stayed? Why didn't he ring?'

'He rang this morning,' said Susannah casually. 'Said he'd be delayed a while. Don't worry,' she added. 'Nothing unusual.'

'Oh!' Mandy sat down, the wind taken out of her sails. She smiled. 'That's all right, then.'

Except that she waited all day without a word from Pascal. And the next day. And the next. Mandy's heart leapt at every sound till her nerves made her emotional and jumpy. His aunt, unusually irritable and snappy, protested her ignorance of his whereabouts and said that she didn't know the names or addresses of any of his friends or business acquaintances.

Something was wrong. She was sure that Susannah knew something.

On the fourth day Mandy stood on the cliff, watching for a sign of the little dugout, hoping to see it speeding over the waves at that perilous angle it adopted whenever it changed direction.

And she became afraid. Pascal knew the coast like the back of his hand but it was dangerous. Sudden gusts of wind could cause trouble, vicious currents could suck a boat towards the rock cliffs...engines could fail. Even

the one on the well-maintained yacht had gone wrong.
If the pirogue outboard motor had failed, especially
during the night, Pascal would be in trouble.

Frantic with worry, she decided to ring the police.
Walking back to the house through the lush garden, she
thought that if anything had happened to him all this
beauty would be as nothing to her. She'd trade all of
that and the wealth in exchange for Pascal. Sobs of terror
shook her body. If he never came back she would have
so much, but so little. Her child, yes, but she would
have lost her friend, her lover, her beloved husband.

In a miraculously short time they had become bonded
together so closely that a part of her would be torn away
if he...if he... 'Oh, Pascal!' she groaned, stumbling
blindly.

A hand caught her and she gasped in hope but knew
even before she saw Anseydit that it wasn't Pascal's—
she knew his hand too well, had kissed it and held it and
loved it.

'I nearly done the cradle,' said Anseydit in his musical
voice. 'I was talkin' to my sister in Anse La Verdure
Hotel this mornin' and I saw Mr Pascal. He said—'

'What? Wait a minute!' Mandy said urgently. 'You
saw him in the hotel? This morning?'

'Yes, he—'

'How did you get there?' she demanded excitedly. 'We
haven't any boats—'

'My cousin, Chardonnay,' said the puzzled Anseydit.
'He's come to see the cradle. We went to visit my sister
and—'

'Anseydit,' broke in Mandy hastily, 'is he still here?
Can he take me to Anse La Verdure beach?'

'Sure he can, Miss Mandy!' beamed the carpenter.
'Maybe you can cheer Mr Pascal up. He bit my head
off and that surprised me, I can tell you.'

She bit her lip. Something *was* wrong. But he was alive!
Of course he was. How stupid she'd been! She beamed.

'Thank you,' she said warmly. 'And when we get back we'd love to see the cradle. Thank you, Anseydit. I'm very grateful.'

'No problem, no problem.'

And he introduced Mandy to his cousin who cheerfully helped her into the boat then set off for the beach to the south.

'Mr Pascal said he was going up to Reception,' said Anseydit's cousin helpfully, when he'd driven the boat up onto the beach.

Mandy thanked him and asked him to wait, and the man good-naturedly nodded and drew his hat over his face, settling down to a sleep in the sun. She splashed through the shallows and made her way to Reception.

'Hello, Bertha! Hello, Dianne,' she cried brightly. 'Isn't it...?' She paused and frowned. The two women looked horrified. 'What is it?' she asked in agitation. 'What's the matter? Pascal? Tell me! Tell me!' she cried.

'I—I don't know...' Bertha goggled at Dianne. 'I'll get someone to fetch him,' she said hastily.

'No.' Mandy felt a chill run through her. The women were behaving furtively. A brief and terrifying fear of possible infidelity sped through her mind but she crushed it. Pascal loved her. But the women were panic-stricken. They had that *look* about them. And she trembled. 'He's... all right?' she asked tentatively.

'Yes, yes, fine!' nodded Bertha with too much fervour. 'One of the lads will fetch him from—' Her mouth shut like a steel trap.

'Where is he?' she said nervously. *'Where is he?'*

'He's had to see someone—'

'Who?' she snapped.

'Simon will take you,' said Bertha quietly.

Mandy whirled around. Simon was standing behind her, his mouth working with distress. 'Show me,' she breathed.

Without a word Simon walked up the hill to the highest, most luxurious villas, built with open sides so that the light breezes could drift through the rooms. Built so that she could hear voices as she came up the path—one of them Pascal's, the other a woman's.

'Leave me,' she whispered to Simon. The young man scampered down the hill as if glad to go. She walked to the panelled door and found that it was ajar. Her heart was thudding violently, her nerves at screaming point. He couldn't. He wouldn't. He loved her. She *knew* he loved her.

Inside was a flight of steps. She climbed up them like an old woman, the life ebbing from her body. A huge room was ahead, the paddle fans whirring overhead. Clothes lay strewn on the floor in a trail as if they'd been shed piece by piece by a lover. Cold shivers chased down her spine.

On her right she could see the unmade bed and a satin nightdress. She could hardly breathe. The voices were low, urgent and came from the deck, which was half-hidden by a huge jalousie screen.

She pressed one hand to her heart, the other to her stomach where her baby lay. Their baby. Instinct told her to flee, to remain in ignorance and to pretend that she believed him when he told her where he'd been. The need to know the truth forced her forward, slowly, over the cool, tiled floor.

A woman came into view—a blonde woman, frightened, pressed flat against a pillar. Mandy froze. The woman was more beautiful than any woman she'd ever seen, with a kind of Grace Kelly beauty of regal purity. Her face was strangely familiar, the stunning bone-structure so perfect that men would be unable to take their eyes off her. She wore a towelling robe and nothing else.

That was obvious because a half-naked Pascal was holding the woman's bare shoulders where her robe had been wrenched away...in passion? Mandy gulped. His eyes were blazing and intent. The woman was gasping as if short of breath, and one long, tanned leg was exposed to the upper thigh where the robe had parted.

She saw nothing more. The room spun dizzyingly. 'Pascal!' she rasped in blind horror. 'Pascal!'

His head whipped around and she saw the blur as he rushed forward and the room began to grow dim...

When she came around from her faint she found herself lying on the ground outside in the shade of a nutmeg tree, being gently fanned by Pascal.

'Mandy,' he growled. 'Are you all right?'

'No!' she yelled, sitting up too quickly and swaying alarmingly. He steadied her but she pushed him away. 'Don't touch me!' she raged. 'Look at you! Naked to the waist! Where have you been all this time? Don't you know I was half-crazy with worry? How could you do this to me? How could you?'

He drew back and stood up. She saw that he looked terrible, as if he hadn't shaved since he'd left home. No, it was more than that. As if he had been locked in a dark hell and they'd thrown away the key. She gave a strangled sob. Maybe he knew that she'd leave him if he'd been unfaithful. And that she would take their child.

'I'm sorry,' he said harshly. 'Mandy—'

'That woman!' she said hoarsely. 'Were you and she...?' Her eyes closed. Sickness soured her stomach. 'Were you...?'

His eyes, bleak and glacial, flicked up to hers and then he looked away as if he was too ashamed of his guilt. 'I—' His white teeth clenched savagely when she began to sob quietly. 'Yes. Yes, we were. I was with her. Don't play the wronged wife,' he muttered. 'I had to. I—I had to get away. I needed variety.'

He turned his back on her, his hand gripping a branch of the tree. It snapped and he looked at it as if puzzled that he'd exerted so much strength on it. 'I'll do this

from time to time,' he said, as if it cost him a great deal
to admit his weakness. 'I've been . . . doing it ever since
we met.'

He swung around and it seemed to her appalled eyes
that it was a cold, emotionless statue telling her these
awful things. 'I need—women,' he said jerkily. 'Plenty
of women. All kinds, all shapes, all sizes,' he growled.
'Get used to it. Or go.'

CHAPTER NINE

SLOWLY, and with great difficulty, Mandy stood up. Pride kept her from falling; dignity and shock held her rigid. Pascal had betrayed her—and he wasn't at all repentant. There would be many other women in his life and Susannah had known this; everyone had known and only she had been blindly trusting.

She wanted to scream and tear his clothes, to score her nails down his stony face. But she knew that if she did that she would go mad. And so she held in the horror, closed her heart to anyone but her unborn child, and made herself a silent promise never to trust anyone for the rest of her life.

The light was falling in shafts through the foliage above him and she remembered their first meeting, where he'd lain like a basking tiger, waiting for his prey. Her first impressions had been right. He was dangerous and he could bite. Like his amoral father.

'Blood will out,' she husked, holding her chin high.

He winced as if she'd whipped him. 'Yes,' he muttered.

'You rat!'

'Mandy—'

'No!' She waved him away with a jerk of her hand.

She felt a roaring in her ears and she dug her nails into her palms so that she might keep from showing any weakness. Somehow she managed to walk away from him, every step an immense effort, every beat of her heart taking her from the man she'd loved and trusted.

He'd opened a wound and it would never be healed. She remembered that he'd half warned her when he'd said that he couldn't love another woman in the way

170

he'd loved his first wife. The rest, the protestations of love when she'd told him about their baby, had been empty lies.

When she was several yards from him she swivelled around, her face pale beneath her golden tan. 'For the second time, your wife won't be saying goodbye,' she called in clear, ringing tones. 'You're not worth the courtesy.'

He didn't move a muscle and it almost broke her to see the man she'd loved so stonily indifferent to her misery. A spasm of pure pain seared her body with the viciousness of a slicing knife and she gave an involuntary moan. Pascal and she turned away from one another sharply.

Without knowing how she remained on her feet she walked down the hill, past the two concerned women in Reception, and climbed into the boat. 'Beau Jardin,' she whispered. It wasn't home. Not any more.

She pushed past the startled Anseydit when they landed, her tears threatening to engulf her before she reached the safety of her bedroom. But Anseydit ran beside her, jabbering rapidly, pointing to a launch in the bay. Suddenly she registered what he was saying—that Pascal's father was on the veranda.

At the very edge of hysteria, she walked up the wooden steps, her unhappy eyes on the thin, frail man with thinning grey hair who lay weakly on a steamer chair, his legs wrapped in a cashmere rug. He could only be in his early sixties yet his face was dissipated and weary, with lines of pain etched deeply around his mouth and in the clefts between his brows. Once he must have been a handsome man; the watery brown eyes still retained some of their command.

'He's not here,' she said coldly.

'I can see that,' he snapped. 'Who the hell are you?' he asked hoarsely.

She hesitated. Suddenly she didn't feel married. 'Mandy Cook.'

'Mandy!' A slow, delighted smile touched his face. 'Mandy! I'm delighted to meet you at last! Please, let's talk...' He coughed—a terrible racking cough that seemed to paralyse him—and Mandy, after a moment's hesitation, hurried forward and anxiously put a glass of water to his lips.

'You should be in hospital,' she muttered. 'What are you doing here?'

'I had to see you,' he grated, when the fit was over. 'Damn lungs! Them or my liver'll be the death of me yet.' His hard, rough, nicotine-stained hand gripped her wrist like a vice. 'I had to see you before Pascal got rid of you. I don't trust him an inch!'

'Neither do I!' she grated. She remembered what Vincente had wanted to do with her and tried to break free, filled with loathing for the St Honoré men. They thought they could manipulate women, use them for their own needs!

'Hold still! I want to look at you!'

'No,' she said in disgust. 'Let me go!'

The merciless hand drew her closer and he scanned her face in detail. 'You're not like her. Not in any way.'

'Like who?' she asked, with a frown.

'Mary.'

Mandy tried to hold onto her patience. The man was sick. Possibly hallucinating. 'Mary who?' she asked.

'My wife,' sighed Vincente confusingly. 'Susannah says Pascal is still in a furious temper. Sulking, I suppose. What pretty hands you have. I see you're married. Is your husband with you?'

This was farcical. She had to get away. Yet his remark arrested her. 'No. He's not. And...why would Pascal have been sulking?' she asked warily.

Vincente touched her hair and she would have jerked back, but there was a gentle love in his eyes that she couldn't fathom because it was definitely not sexual. Perhaps, she thought bitterly, Pascal had told his father about them and the baby, and Vincente's hostility had vanished at the thought of a grandchild. And she felt a twinge of pity for him because it was too late for playing happy families.

'He's mad because I told him a while ago that I was going to disinherit him,' he chuckled nastily. 'I told him that as I was being loaded into the ambulance. It made me feel a lot better. I said he had to meet you and treat you well because I was going to leave everything to you. I've remade my will in your favour, Mandy. You're my heir. Are you pleased, my dear?'

She froze. Vincente continued to smile smugly at her while her mind sought to make sense of what he'd said. 'You're ill,' she said gently. 'The drugs—'

'No. I haven't been taking their damn drugs! Ask Susannah. She's disappeared somewhere but she knows. I told Pascal about my new will as they were closing the ambulance doors and he ran after it, yelling and banging on the doors,' said Vincente with satisfaction. 'Only seen him that angry once before and he attacked me then.'

Mandy felt herself trembling when she recalled that Pascal had said that his father had threatened to leave Beau Rivage to his mistress. It was true. Impossible, irrational but... true!

She tried to understand the implications. Pascal had known at the time he'd first met her that she, a stranger, for some crazy, illogical reason, had been named as his father's beneficiary.

That was why he'd tried to get rid of her. Why he'd done his best to damn her reputation and send her home squirming with embarrassment and shame. And he'd failed; that was why he'd... Her eyes flickered with pain.

Then he'd married her. It was so obvious now she thought of it. Marriage had been the only option left if he was to keep the land he desired with every fibre of his being.

Between them the two St Honoré men had ruined her life. 'You malicious old man!' she screamed, snatching her hand away in horror. 'You wanted to avenge yourself on your son and you didn't care who was hurt in the process! You don't know; you can't have any idea of what you've done to me!'

'Mandy! Mandy!' he quavered hoarsely.

But she ran furiously into the house, to her room, where she began to fling her clothes into a suitcase. Her shaking hand snatched open the drawer where her undies were kept and then she stopped, aghast. Sitting prettily on a bed of soft oyster satin were the little baby booties that Pascal had given her as their baby's first present.

It was too much to bear. Mandy finally gave way. She crumpled to the ground and wept. She would go home. She would beg for her old job back and become a statistic—another single mother. Her child would be without a father and she would live a life without adult love.

She sobbed loudly, knowing that she could have borne all of that if Pascal had never woken her heart. But he'd shown her the deep joy of true love and for that she cursed him. He'd woken her and yet had remained untouched, a sleeping tiger with only an animal's instincts for life—for food and sex.

He'd lied to her from the very beginning, knowing that she was a serious threat. All he'd ever wanted was to secure his future from his dying father, and to win the terrible game of revenge that the two men were playing to the death. Pascal would have kept her from seeing his father, hoping that he would die. She shuddered. It was horrible. Revolting.

'I've come to take you to the airport,' came a voice from behind her.

Mandy sucked in her breath and held it as the soft, seductive voice whispered through her raw body, jangling every nerve. She wanted to run to him, throw herself into his arms and seek comfort there. Fiercely she pulled her mind back from lurching to the brink of stupidity and steadied her pulses. She turned around.

'Why didn't you have the decency to let me leave without seeing me again? I didn't expect you to come back, Pascal!' she said bitterly.

'It's my home.'

She winced at the cold, deadpan delivery. He felt nothing. *Nothing!* 'I don't want you near me,' she muttered in disgust.

'I'm not touching you, am I? And I won't let anyone else take you,' he growled. 'If you want to leave St Lucia, then I'm more than willing to help you on your way.'

'My God! You said you could be hard and ruthless,' she said furiously. 'I never realised how hard, how ruthless! I only hope to God that my child doesn't carry too many of your genes! If I knew that he or she would turn out like you or your father—'

'I'll take your luggage.'

Mandy felt like hitting him—anything to get a re-action—because she felt as if a steamroller had hit her and he might have had the decency to be a *little* upset.

'Have you seen your father? Is he still sitting on the veranda?' she asked curtly.

He tensed. Knowing him so well—or so she'd thought—she was sure that she had startled him. 'The boat! I thought one of the staff must be here... It's Father? He's...*here*?'

'Yes,' she snapped.

'He must have discharged himself! Typical. Stubborn fool,' he muttered furiously. He slanted a cautious glance at her. 'Did he...did he talk to you?' he asked carefully.

'Oh, yes!' she scathed, her mouth tightening when Pascal took a sharp breath. 'He told me that you knew before we ever met that I was to inherit Beau Rivage! So now I understand why you were hostile to me. I know why you decided to marry me. You might have wanted sex but you certainly wanted to keep your inheritance too, didn't you?'

'I want Rivage, yes. I wanted sex.' He hesitated, his face suddenly haggard. 'Did he say... anything... else?'

'Isn't that enough? He's crazy!' she snapped. 'It's mad to leave a plantation to a strange woman you intend to make your mistress!'

The breath hissed out of Pascal's body, almost as if in relief, and the tension in his high shoulders slipped away.

'Well, don't worry. I'm not accepting. It would mean being your neighbour! *You* tell him he can keep his plantation and give it to someone else! I don't want to see him again. Make sure he's gone before I step out of here.'

'I'll do that all right! Wait. I'll get rid of him,' he said savagely.

After he'd stormed out she lifted her hand to the linen hangings on the bed for much needed support. She felt weak, but she had to be strong. Ahead of her was an hour and a half's journey to the airport—with Pascal. And then the journey home. And then...

Somewhere outside in the garden Pascal was shouting his father's name impatiently, as if Vincente was proving difficult to find. Almost sagging with emotional exhaustion, she wearily picked up her flight bag and took it out to the landing. And came face to face with Vincente himself.

'Oh, no!' she groaned.

'Mandy,' he said in a soft, gravelly plea.

'No!' she said sharply, recoiling from his outstretched arms. 'Get away from me! I loathe you both—'

'You can't!' wailed Vincente. 'You can't loathe me! I've spent the last few years searching for you! I've paid out thousands of dollars—'

'You wasted your time trying to find the perfect mistress of Beau Rivage,' she snapped. 'I can't be bought.

I'd rather suffer poverty in England than the kind of life you lead.'

'But... Lacey said you were absolutely desperate to find your family. Hasn't Pascal told you about you and me?' asked Vincente.

'Yes,' she said tersely. 'I'm your mail-order mistress.'

Vincente gaped. 'Nothing could be further from the truth! I'm your father, Mandy!'

'You're *mad*!' she gasped, staggering back. She came into contact with a hard, unyielding body and jumped away because she knew it was Pascal. She pressed herself against the wall, her huge, horrified eyes darting from one man to the other. Both a little crazy. Both torturing her...

'Tell her, Pascal!' grated Vincente. 'Tell her she's my daughter!'

Angrily Mandy opened her mouth to speak. But the furious words died in her throat. Pascal was staring at her, his face ashen. 'No,' she whispered, refusing to accept what she saw. *'No!'*

'Tell her!' bellowed his father. 'You know it's true. I told you several days ago that she's my daughter!'

Mandy started. That was when Pascal had disappeared. 'Vincente... you mean you advertised for me...because you had discovered...' She swallowed the choking lump in her throat. It was hard to say. 'You thought I might be your daughter?' she croaked.

'That's right,' Vincente said, 'but the investigators couldn't find you anywhere. You'd vanished from Glasgow—'

'Dave and I went to Devon when we married,' she whispered.

'The agency I hired was chasing dead ends for months. I finally resorted to advertising for you because I'm dying. I wanted to see you as mistress of Beau Rivage before I go.'

Mandy stared, wide-eyed, in shock at Pascal. To have Vincente as a father...

'I have proof,' persisted Vincente. 'Mary, my wife—your mother—ran away twenty-six years ago. She left a note saying she was pregnant, knowing it would twist the knife in the wound for me. I'd wanted children for years,' he said bitterly. 'We traced Mary to the Sunnyside nursing home in Glasgow. The detective agency has told me that you are registered as her child. We followed the trail to the two children's homes where you stayed and then it petered out after your marriage. It's taken me a long time to find you but there's no doubt. You're Mary's daughter. Mine.'

Mandy blinked in horror as something dawned on her. If this was so, she was Pascal's sister.

His sister and his wife.

'No!' she said hoarsely. 'It isn't possible!'

'There's no doubt,' protested Vincente.

One of Mandy's wildly shaking hands stole to her stomach. With the other she slowly removed her wedding ring. Pascal seemed turned to stone. No emotion showed on his face. *He knew,* she thought. And he'd been too chicken to tell her.

Shaking badly, she dropped the ring at his feet and walked down the stairs, her feet echoing on the fragrant, beeswaxed treads in the deathly silence that had fallen.

Susannah emerged from the shadows of the library and ran forward, catching Mandy by the wrist in an astonishingly fierce grip. 'Mandy! Wait! I heard everything. But Pascal isn't your brother—'

'You're only *saying* that!' Mandy sobbed, twisting her arm free. '*They* know. They believe it!' she wailed, pointing a shaking finger at the top of the stairs.

'Mandy—'

'*No!*'

She fled outside, her hands over her ears. Beyond that, she didn't know what she was going to do. But her prime instinct was to hide from all eyes, to shut herself away from anyone who might point at her and whisper the word 'incest'.

So she ran. Faster than she ever had in her life, because her life was running after her, chasing her with its horrors, coming at her from all directions and screaming dreadful things in her ears. Blanking her mind, thinking only of where her feet landed, she raced along a jungle path without heeding the boa constrictors or other dangers, startling pigeons and grackles and kingbirds, bleeding from where her legs and arms had been torn by sharp branches, not caring and hardly feeling any physical pain because her mind had become filled to bursting with all the pain in the world.

She might be guilty of loving her brother. Knowing him biblically, forming his child within her. At long last a terrified wail broke out from her anguished chest. This was the child she had planned on devoting her life to! Her baby was to have been her only love, the only piece of the world she could trust!

The pain in her side suddenly stopped her from breaking. Exhausted, she leaned against the trunk of a flame-tree. Her child was all she had. But... Her head tipped back and the tears streamed down her face.

Her anguished cry rent the air and there was a tremendous flapping of wings as the birds fled from the shelter of the trees around her. The sky was a deep, searing blue between the fanned branches above and the bright scarlet flowers on the flame-tree looked like bursts of fireworks.

Pained by the beauty she saw, she gazed miserably instead at the forest floor. Her heart was breaking.

'What shall I do?' she said aloud in total despair. 'Oh, help me, someone!'

She heard a crashing sound from back down the path and knew that it must be Pascal. But she was too tired and too listless to run any more. Nothing worse could happen to her. What did anything matter now?

The hurrying feet stopped. 'We are not brother and sister,' came Pascal's voice, strong with confidence, laced with a hurting compassion. She turned her head in a hopeless gesture, refusing to listen. 'Susannah assures me we're not. Father is lying for some foul purpose.' She kept her head bowed. 'He was so convincing that I believed him when he told me you were his daughter a few days ago. That's why I didn't come back home.'

'And why you found solace in another woman's arms?' she demanded brutally, wanting him to be hurt too.

He winced. 'Do you think I could possibly contemplate sex after what I'd discovered?' he replied.

'I could believe anything of you,' she said rawly.

'Mandy!' he said in a helpless tone. 'I was trying to do what was best! After Father told me, I went to Anse La Verdure Hotel and never left my villa. I paced up and down for hour after hour, trying to work out what to do—'

'The blonde was a figment of my imagination?' she cried waspishly.

'No. One of the girls in Reception came to tell me that she'd been asking for my father. I was trying to find out what the woman wanted when you turned up.'

Mandy flushed, remembering. 'You were half-naked! Her clothes—'

'Mandy!' he said in exasperation. 'I'd been sitting in my villa when I was told this woman wanted to see Father. I didn't stop to change or put on a shirt. It is a beach resort, you know! And I interrupted her shower, I think. She answered the door in her robe and I pushed past her and began to interrogate her.

'When you accused me of infidelity, I decided it was my way out. I would behave brutally towards you so that you'd want to leave me. And you'd never find out the truth. I couldn't bear you to know. My infidelity seemed the lesser of the two evils.'

His words sank in. 'You thought it was true, then.'

'I did. Not any more.'

She looked up, wanting to believe that. 'Why not?'

'Susannah ran after me just now,' he said quietly. 'I was more interested in finding you, but she was yelling something about it being all right. That we weren't related and we mustn't worry. Maybe she knows something no one else does. She was very close to my mother so we can find out. I want you to come back and talk to Susannah,' he said gravely. 'We can't just part without knowing for certain. We can't give up what we had—'

'Your father was so sure—' she began.

'Every instinct in my body tells me not to believe it,' he replied, his tone strong and convincing.

She hugged herself tightly, her pale face stained with tears. 'Why did you try to prevent me from knowing?' she asked shakily.

He gave a ghost of a smile. 'Because I love you. I love you so much that I'd do anything to protect you.'

The gentle, adoring tone pierced her like a knife. 'Oh, Pascal!' she sighed brokenly, and knew that she loved him still. And then she knew that they couldn't be related. It was impossible.

'You're everything to me,' he said thickly. 'I trust Susannah. Not Father. In my heart I *know* he's made a mistake—or the detective agency has. But, whatever the truth, I want to protect you and care for you more than anything in the world and I would do anything to save you from the way you are feeling now.'

She reeled at his impassioned words and her fuddled mind cleared as if it had been swept by a broom. Remembering the agony in his face when he had told her that he would always be unfaithful, she felt her heart contract. That had been an act of love. He'd put himself in a bad light so that she wouldn't be hurt.

'I love you,' he said soberly.

They couldn't be related. They just couldn't.

Her mouth trembled because she wanted to believe that there was a mistake and she feared that maybe it was blind hope that was telling her these things.

She groaned. At last she met his eyes, and wished that she hadn't. He was hurting as much as she was and it made her sob to see him so distressed. He had taken her in his arms before she could stop him. He was holding her as if he never wanted her to leave.

'Come back to the house,' he said gently. 'We have to question Susannah—and also the research. Father's detectives have come up with more than mine have and that surprises me. My people are thorough. Walk back and I'll tell you what I know.'

'Your father said that his wife was pregnant when she left here,' she said as they began to make their way through the forest.

'Yes. Mother disappeared and he washed his hands of her—and his child—till he learnt how ill he was. When I went to visit him a few days ago he showed me the correspondence between him and the detective agency. It seems that your mother was a Mary Brandon. *My* mother was called Mary too. She was the daughter of the Earl of Castlestowe, whose family seat is in Scotland. And after she disappeared she was traced to the Sunnyside nursing home.'

He frowned. 'However, I've only had a cursory glance at the agency's report—and I was stunned at the time and not thinking straight. I'd like to go through it carefully.'

'But...I couldn't *possibly* be from a titled family!' she demurred. 'Maybe there was a switch of those labels they put on babies' wrists.' Even as she said that she realised that she was grasping at straws. But her conviction that an error had been made was growing. She loved Pascal and not as a brother.

'Who knows?' Pascal said. 'Anything's possible. Apparently Father had used Lacey's partner when he'd advertised for "companions" and he tried the same people and the same method to find you. In a way, I wish you *had* been destined for his bed,' he muttered. 'That I could have coped with.'

'I must know the truth,' she said in a small voice.

'We'll get you a DNA test as soon as possible. I know that the waiting will kill me.' His hands clenched into fists. 'I'd give anything not to hurt you! You've been through so much—'

'And you,' she said tremulously. Nausea was filling her stomach, swelling inside her like a foul poison. 'I'm going to be sick,' she whispered, and she retched till she thought that her body would split in two.

Pascal held her shoulders all the time, encouraging her, soothing her, gentling her. 'I love you,' he said. 'I will take care of you and protect you. Trust me.' He took out his handkerchief and tenderly wiped her face, then picked her up in his arms and grimly strode back to the house.

'What the hell's up with her?' said Vincente irritably when they appeared.

'I think you'd better go,' snarled Pascal, his face savage with anger, 'before I'm tempted to throttle you.'

'Because she's my daughter?' taunted the old man. 'Or because you're not my son?'

Mandy found herself slipping from Pascal's lifeless arms. Almost absently he set her on her feet, his eyes narrowed and wary. '*What* was that?' he asked menacingly.

Vincente smirked. 'I thought that would take the arrogant sneer off your face. You're not my son, Pascal. Now that my legitimate heir has turned up I can tell you that. You're a bastard. Your mother and I were married for six years with no sign of a son. I wanted one. You were...available. But neither I nor Mary gave you life. There's no blood of mine in your veins.'

Mandy gasped. Susannah had been right! There was no problem! 'We're not...brother and sister?' she said. A ton of guilt and despair lifted from her like a curtain. She'd never imagined it would be *that* way round—that *she* would prove to be Vincente's legitimate child, whereas Pascal... 'Pascal—'

But already he was lifting her into the air, laughing with her, kissing her. And then she found herself crushed to his breast, his heart racing as wildly as hers. They were not brother and sister. And at that moment those were the most wonderful words in the world.

'What the hell are you doing, Pascal? Aren't you upset?' growled Vincente angrily.

'No!' Pascal laughed. His hand stroked Mandy's hair and he looked into her eyes. 'Delighted.'

Vincente's face twisted in rage. 'Don't think I'm going to tell you who your parents are! You can whistle for that information!'

'Frankly,' said Pascal, 'I don't give a damn.'

'You won't get Beau Rivage!' raged his father. 'It'll be given to Mandy and her husband!'

'Suits me.' Pascal smiled at Mandy, his eyes bright with their secret. 'I think you need a celebratory drink, darling. I certainly do. Champagne?'

'Champagne,' she breathed, her eyes alight with joy. She could live again, love again.

They stole away from the house, tiptoeing down to the gazebo on the beach. They heard Vincente ranting around the house and garden, yelling himself hoarse, then the sound of Vincente's launch leaving the bay.

When the throb of the engine had died away, Pascal lit the hurricane lamps in their love-nest.

'Oh, Pascal, I can't believe it!' she cried passionately.

'Nor I.' His voice was shaky and his eyelashes were suspiciously wet.

Mandy watched him opening the champagne and wondered briefly whether Susannah was his mother—but remembered almost immediately that Susannah would have been only fifteen or sixteen when he was born.

'It's funny,' she mused. 'It's possible that I've found my parents after a lifetime of searching—and I'm not sure I'm too pleased about it. You've lost both of yours and you don't care at all!'

'But that's because we nearly lost something much more precious,' he said softly. 'Each other.' He put down the two glasses and came to kiss her. 'And, now we haven't, everything else pales into insignificance.'

'I'll say!' She gave a little shudder. 'When I thought you'd betrayed me my world came tumbling about my ears. I'll never forget how I felt. The shock—'

'I'm sorry, darling,' he said fervently. 'It hurt me to inflict such pain on you. But I couldn't tell you what I thought to be the truth. I couldn't let you live with that horror. I thought it better that you should hate and despise me—and perhaps find someone else to love. But it broke my heart to cause you distress,' he admitted.

She stroked his face and smoothed out the lines of anguish as he remembered that terrible moment. 'I doubt I'd ever have fallen in love so deeply again.'

Pascal squeezed her tightly as though he needed to release some of his heartfelt relief. 'Father's revelation seemed to fulfil a fear I'd had ever since I fell in love with you. On our honeymoon, you see, I had this feeling of dread,' he mused in her ear. 'Paranoiac, I know, but everything seemed too good to be true and I was half-afraid that I'd wake up one morning and you'd be gone. A figment of my imagination.'

'My feelings exactly!' she exclaimed in surprise, and they looked at one another, smiling ruefully. 'I could hardly believe my luck. For me, you were everything. I didn't dare to think that you loved me as completely as I love you.'

'But I do.' He touched her hair where a shaft of sun burnished it to a rich mahogany. 'When I think of you, I smile—'

'Giggle, you mean?' she teased, so secure now that she could pretend to be offended.

He took her hands in his, turned them over and kissed each palm reverently. 'Smile,' he repeated with mock severity, and then his eyes twinkled. 'You must have seen how happy I was, how I went about with a permanent grin on my face!' He gave a throaty chuckle. 'You've made me laugh again...' She raised an eyebrow, as if hurt, and he tapped her nose in fond reproof. 'You know what I mean!' he protested.

'Yes,' she said happily, knowing that she had found laughter too, after years of sadness. 'I do.'

Pascal touched his lips to hers. 'Knowing you're my wife gives me a feeling of warm happiness inside. When I'm away from you, I want to hurry back to you,' he said passionately. 'When I'm with you, I'm content. You're my friend, my lover, my wife, the mother of our baby. I love you so much, Mandy. I will never leave you,' he promised. 'Or our child.'

'Nor I you. We have each other and we have Beau Jardin. We have our child.'

He nodded. 'With you, Beau Jardin and our baby, I feel as contented as—'

'A honey-fed tiger,' she supplied with a giggle.

'Feed me honey,' he murmured wickedly. 'I'm tempted to devour you. Keep me sweet.'

Tenderly he kissed her throat and her breasts. Mandy shuddered and surrender herself in delight to her beloved husband's passion.

* * * * *

Look out for Ginny's story in SCARLET LADY, available next month.

HARLEQUIN WOMEN KNOW ROMANCE WHEN THEY SEE IT.

Take 4 bestselling love stories FREE

Plus get a FREE surprise gift!

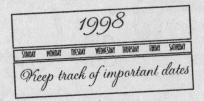

1998

SUNDAY   MONDAY   TUESDAY   WEDNESDAY   THURSDAY   FRIDAY   SATURDAY

Keep track of important dates

Three beautiful and colorful calendars that celebrate some of the most popular trends in America today.

Look for:

Just Babies—a 16 month calendar that features a full year of absolutely adorable babies!

1998 CALENDAR
Just Babies
16 months of adorable bundles of joy!

Hometown Quilts
1998 Calendar
A 16 month quilting extravaganza!

Hometown Quilts—a 16 month calendar featuring quilted art squares, plus a short history on twelve different quilt patterns.

Inspirations—a 16 month calendar with inspiring pictures and quotations.

Inspirations

A 16 month calendar that will lift your spirits and gladden your heart

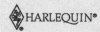

Steeple Hill™   ◆ HARLEQUIN®

Value priced at $9.99 U.S./$11.99 CAN., these calendars make a perfect gift!

Available in retail outlets in August 1997.   CAL98

As Seen on TV!

Free Gift Offer

With a Free Gift proof-of-purchase
from any Harlequin® book, you can receive
a beautiful cubic zirconia pendant.

This stunning marquise-shaped stone is a genuine cubic
zirconia—accented by an 18" gold tone necklace.
(Approximate retail value $19.95)

Send for yours today...
compliments of ◈ HARLEQUIN®

To receive your free gift, a cubic zirconia pendant, send us one original proof-of-purchase, photocopies not accepted, from the back of any Harlequin Romance®, Harlequin Presents®, Harlequin Temptation®, Harlequin Superromance®, Harlequin Intrigue®, Harlequin American Romance®, or Harlequin Historicals® title available at your favorite retail outlet, together with the Free Gift Certificate, plus a check or money order for $1.65 U.S./$2.15 CAN. (do not send cash) to cover postage and handling, payable to Harlequin Free Gift Offer. We will send you the specified gift. Allow 6 to 8 weeks for delivery. Offer good until December 31, 1997, or while quantities last. Offer valid in the U.S. and Canada only.

Free Gift Certificate

Name: _____

Address: _____

City: _____ State/Province: _____ Zip/Postal Code: _____

Mail this certificate, one proof-of-purchase and a check or money order for postage and handling to: HARLEQUIN FREE GIFT OFFER 1997. In the U.S.: 3010 Walden Avenue, P.O. Box 9071, Buffalo NY 14269-9057. In Canada: P.O. Box 604, Fort Erie, Ontario L2Z 5X3.

FREE GIFT OFFER
084-KEZ

ONE PROOF-OF-PURCHASE
To collect your fabulous FREE GIFT, a cubic zirconia pendant, you must include this
original proof-of-purchase for each gift with the properly completed Free Gift Certificate.

084-KEZR